KINSMAN AVENUE PUBLISHING, INC.
www.kinsmanquarterly.org

Decorum
Author: Nicole Negrón

Edited & Designed by: Monique Franz
Co-Editor: Sophia O. Ofuokwu

DECORUM

A NOVEL

Nicole Negrón

Table of Contents

Table of Contents, cont.

*To my moon, Justice,
and my sun, Charles.*

Chapter 1

Marigold

Marigold's mouth was dry as chalk dust, and her heart pounded as she tried to remember how she got home. She took a wobbly step out of bed, making her way through the hall, when she stumbled over a large lump in the middle of the floor. She looked down, and her breath caught in her throat. Marigold stumbled backward, landing hard on her hands and tailbone. Trembling, she crab-walked back into her bedroom—cursing and sobbing. Darkness crept into the corners of her eyes, her vision tunneling, and only the buzz of her phone alarm kept her from fading completely.

There's just no way. Marigold wanted to believe it was all a dream but glanced over and saw her meds sitting beside an empty bottle of Merlot.

Unable to stand, she crawled through her bedroom doorway, slowly back toward the hallway and the body. When she got close, her hands floated upward, yanking at her auburn hair. She began to rock gently, convulsing as she took in Alberto's shell on the floor. His face, caked in blood—the slack of his jaw taunted her from its position until she couldn't stand it any longer.

She rushed to her bed, yanked off the duvet, and ran to the hall. She flung the duvet over his body. When her reeling mind could no longer see his face, she collapsed onto the floor.

Marigold squeezed her eyes shut again, trying to replay the moments before her journey home—the day or night before. The scenes of her last encounter with Alberto blurred together; she could not remember him being in her house at all. *Did I …? What did I do?*

Marigold sprung into action, running barefoot through the house to the large attached garage, where her car sat idle and hidden. Her eyes darted back and forth, searching for the wheelbarrow. Before she could change her mind or truly consider what it meant to move a body, she began dragging Alberto's dead weight across the threshold, dirt ground between her toes.

She tipped the cart, pushed him into the mouth of it, summoning every ounce of her panicked strength to roll him to the back of the car. She popped the trunk, then heaved and heaved to wrestle the body inside. After squeezing his legs the rest of the way in—the shuffle and crunch of which made her gag—she took one last look at the lumps beneath the duvet and closed the trunk with a soft click.

Chapter 2

One week earlier

Solei

Why isn't she answering? Solei thought as she drove along the Cross Valley Expressway toward Dallas, Pennsylvania.

"Mama, it's Solei. I'm coming to help with the office. I'm running late, but I am coming. I have my key. I'll start without you. If you're anywhere near Dunk— " The beep signaled the end of the voicemail. "Dammit."

It read 4:17 p.m. on the car radio, and a tinge of anxiety stirred at her mother's absence. *You're never late, Ma.*

Solei took a few deep breaths, knowing she had to stay as calm as possible for the evening ahead. The order of events— arguing with her mother in Spanglish about what papers to keep, which to shred, and which to discard, then a side-eye before Solei's dismissal. She took a few deep breaths. She didn't mind spending time with her mother, but not when things like paperwork or choices were involved.

Her yellow Jeep rolled down the creekside road, a fall breeze blowing through the open roof. Pulling around the bend, she felt a pang of nostalgia as her childhood home came into view. The white rocking chair on the wraparound porch bobbed back and forth as if someone had just sat there. Their Victorian was aglow in all its pastel hues—as eclectic as her mother, Luz, could get. Some thirty years ago, she had conceded to her husband's whims that it had character. As far as Solei knew, that was the only concession her mother had ever made, which made her a perfect fit for her father.

Solei's artsy dad, Alberto, was described by his friends as a hippie, a description Luz had always scoffed at.

"Could a hippie take a custom perfume shop and turn it into a million-dollar franchise?" she would question as though insulted.

Luz, a type-A woman, always "forgot" to mention she—his wife and partner—had an MBA from Wharton. This rubbed Solei wrong—the way her mother downplayed her role in the business as an equal partner. And all in the name of decorum.

Why was it polite for the husband to be seen as a business tycoon, and his brilliant wife only as the doting homemaker?

"You speak five languages for Pete's sake," Solei would snort aloud.

Solei determined in the eighth grade that she would be a scientist, that was until she found her love of history. Now, she was working on a second master's—this one in Latin American Studies. She was on her way to becoming a "world-renowned museum curator" as her mother phrased it in countless conversations.

"Do I have to be world-renowned?" she sighed. *Pull it together.* She shook off the usual self-deprecating tangent. *Mom's not even here and I'm doing it.*

Solei released her breath as she continued around the front of the house. The drive was devoid of any vehicles. She pulled in, careful not to block, or be blocked in by anyone who might arrive. Anywhere she went, she needed an escape route. Her psychology-obsessed best friend, Camila, would have something to say about that. She frequently used her college training to analyze friends and family.

Solei stood staring at her childhood home, taking in the memories as she scraped her fingernails against her palm. She then opened the creaky door. "Mama, it's me."

No one. Good. I'll have a head start without her obnoxious sighs and snatching.

She walked past the ornate stairwell with carefully chosen family photographs lining the wall. She ignored the slant of the first frame and headed toward her parents' home office.

The door was slightly ajar; a cool breeze made her shudder. Neat rows of boxes stuffed with file folders, envelopes, and other paperwork lined the crème-colored walls. The mahogany desk was clear, except for a folded sheet of sepia paper and envelope; a letter opener was stabbed beside it on the desk.

Solei clicked her tongue, cooed, and chuckled at the thought, then made herself comfortable at the desk. *To read or not to read.* She swiveled side to side in the leather chair. *Just a quick peek.* As she lifted and unfolded the page, a light scent of lavender rose from the paper. *A love letter! It has to be!*

> *Dearest Alberto,*
> *It's been too many years since I've felt you… since you made me that perfume. I understood you wanted to be there for your Solei.*

"What the fuck? Dad?!" Solei's hands began sweating; she wanted to crush the letter. Her dad had always been a loving man who wouldn't hurt a fly. She couldn't even summon an excuse for her father cheating. *How could he do this? I know mom is hard, but…* Solei squeezed her eyes shut until she saw floaters, then read on.

> *I'd love to reminisce, but I need to get it all out while I still have the nerve… and the time. I couldn't fight for you and our child. She wasn't growing up feeling unwanted, but Marigold deserves to know her father, and you her, despite Luz.*
>
> *Did you know I came to your house? That she turned me away, offered me money? That she called our Marigold "the bastard child?" I don't know how you married such a* ▓▓▓*. Here's a photo with Marigold's information on the back.*
>
> *You decide now,*
> *River*

Solei flung the letter across the desk in a huff. She watched it float to the déco rug, not completely sure what to think or how to feel.

A million memories flashed in her mind—times when her father could have disappeared with another woman, missed family events, and there were none… except his long business trips.

What does it matter now anyway? Wait. She shot up from the chair too fast, knocking her knee against the desk and cursing the entire situation. She remembered that a photo was supposed to be enclosed, but the letter seemed poisonous. Solei was afraid to pick it up but had to read the last line again.

"Solei!" Luz yelled from the front door, her voice drifting from the living room toward the kitchen.

Solei scrambled, running her index and middle finger along the inside of the envelope looking for the photo. "Shit, shit!" She hurried to smooth out the letter and envelope, placing them back the way she found them.

She smoothed her skirt and ran her fingers through her hair, not ready to talk about what she found. She needed to process everything.

Mom'll put on the tea kettle. Solei took her phone out of her pocket and snapped a picture of the letter. As water ran in the kitchen, she hurried stealthily down the hall and out of the back door. She could hardly breathe as she got into her car, throwing the gear into drive. Without glancing backward, Solei shot away from the house as fast as she could.

Chapter 3

Camila

Camila answered her phone, straightaway hearing Solei's muted cursings followed by the sound of fists on a steering wheel.

"*Haylo, haylo,*" Camila greeted lightheartedly, prepared to calm her friend down. "Didn't expect the yelling and cursing to commence until much later."

Through what sounded to be clenched teeth, Solei blurted, "I fucking can't! I really freaking can't!"

These words were the besties' call for SOS after Solei saved Camila from a spiked drink at a bar. The phrase was their way of saying *whatever you're doing, stop and help me.*

"You okay driving?" Camila asked.

"I'm fine," Solei replied, a bit more forcefully than the words implied. "Let's meet at the farm, at the picnic area."

"Okay," Camila agreed, worried that Solei might crash. "I'll stay on the line. What's going on?"

Solei worked to explain through heavy sobbing, sniffling, and teeth-clenching—not enough for Camila to understand her words, but enough that she could track Solei's exact arrival.

She scanned the parking lot, perspiration pooling at her lower back as she spotted her friend across the narrow road. Solei's black hair seemed eerily still as she walked in controlled circles around a picnic table. The table stood on the low embankment by the creek, lined with a sparse row of trees—a great place to have a serious conversation.

Camila was often caught in the middle of Solei's family squabbles. Unfortunately, Luz's death grip on her family, along with Alberto's go-with-the-flow attitude, resulted in a daughter who didn't know how to show emotion.

She kept her eyes on Solei as she crossed the small road between the farm's dairy mercantile and the stables. She hadn't understood what Solei was trying to tell her over the phone when she seemed to be hyperventilating into the Bluetooth, but as soon as she was close enough, Camila wrapped her in a big bear hug.

"Let it out," she told her before pulling Solei toward one of the benches farthest from other patrons. "Please, let's sit."

Solei plopped down. Camila swiped at the bench before pulling down on her parka, a barrier between her and the filth.

She began after a cursory look around, "I think it'll help to get grounded before we continue. Take a few deep breaths. Focus on the natural sounds around you; touch the table and focus on that feeling. What do you smell? Once you feel centered, tell me what happened."

Solei looked around, then faced the creek. She closed her eyes as though listening to the water trickle. She took several deep breaths as if honing in on the stimuli, as if blocking out the passersby. After a few seconds, she opened her eyes, unlocked her phone, and thumbed through the gallery. With one more deep breath, she handed Camila the phone.

Camila's eyes widened as her gaze moved across the screen. When finished, she contemplated the best way to enter the conversation. Camila had been teaching Solei how to focus on emotions so she would let them out. She looked around to see only a few scattered people further down the creek, feeding the ducks.

Suddenly, Camila had a flashing memory of Alberto. She pictured *him* in the café—the intimate way that woman touched his arm. It wasn't a daughter's touch.

"Amiga," she ventured.

Solei opened her eyes, "Because an affair wasn't bad enough, but my mother... my mother throwing away any chance... deciding for us all. The letter was dated several months ago. So, everyone has just been lying to me—keeping a sister from me. Neither one of them is going to get away with this. Not this time. What does my mother always tout?"

"Decorum," the two said at the same time.

Solei snatched the phone from Camila's hand. "I'm going to force them to talk to me," she said, typing.

"Remember what we talked about, Solei?" Camila reminded her. "Get it all out, then erase it, and write what you think you'd say if you weren't upset. What you would say if they were standing right in front of you?"

Solei's fingers whirled over the touch screen; her face already hot red.

"Why don't you show me what you want to write?" Camila suggested before moving to read the message— lots of curse words and big feelings. *It's about time.* "Solei, why don't you take a few days to cool down?"

"Okay, okay. The only way to force Luz to talk about anything she doesn't want to talk about is to be rational and calm." Solei said. "How does this sound, 'I know about Marigold…' No, if I mention Marigold, Mom will shut down.

"How about—'I would like to have some family time on Sunday. I could come over at 2:30 p.m. Would that work, Mama?' Specific on the time and day, and my mother's favorite thing—family time."

"Solei, are you listening? We talked about active listening," Camila winced at her own clinical tone, but when Solei was upset, that's all that got through. She was more emotional than Camila had ever seen her.

Solei's phone buzzed.

"Oh God! It's her. Luz is calling," Solei said, panicking.

"Don't answer," Camila replied.

"*Hola*, mama," she answered, putting the call on speakerphone.

"*¿Qué te pasa a ti, niña?*" Luz asked curtly. "There better be a good excuse for leaving the way you did."

"*Lo siento*," Solei answered, rolling her eyes as Luz continued to lecture. Suddenly, Solei blurted, "*Tienes razón*, Mama, I'll come over this week to help. *Lo prometo.*"

Camila stared at her friend with raised eyebrows. There was a shift in her eyes as she hung up with Luz.

"So… what is really happening?" Camila asked.

Solei's voice raised several octaves. "Can you believe she had the nerve to lecture me? Me! She's been lying to my face for years! For literally like—twenty-five freaking years!"

"Solei, *calma*." Camila said, though she wanted Solei to yell, make a scene—something. She looked around at the passersby, feeling the sweat pool on her upper lip.

Solei took a few deep breaths, lowering her voice and looking around. She began doing that thing again— scraping her palms. Then, she closed her eyes as though listening to the bubbling rush of the creek.

Camila watched a soft breeze tousle her hair. Solei's face flushed under the warm sun; the fall leaves fluttered down around her.

"I'm fine. I'm going to my parents' house to snoop around," she replied. "You know, for a second, I actually thought… it doesn't matter."

Chapter 4

Solei

"Mama, it's me," Solei said as she pushed through the front door. She paused, bracing herself for the game of pretend she was about to play. Her mother crossed through the *sala* from the kitchen, looking predictably perfect—white linen pants, a sleeveless turtleneck; her hair set into a neat side ponytail.

Solei squeezed her jaw together tightly. "*Bendición*, Mama," she said, kissing her cheek.

"*Mi hija*, what are you wearing? We're organizing an office, not going to the gym." A brief look of admonishment crossed Luz's face as she waved her tunic-and-tights-clad daughter into the kitchen.

"No, I don't want any tea, Ma," Solei mouthed as her mother turned to offer her a porcelain teacup. Solei knew better and took the cup as she sat on the white leather barstool at the kitchen island. As she feigned drinking, her mother hastily wiped up a nonexistent spill.

The bay window valances had been changed to white sheers with delicate embroidered sunflowers. They complemented the pale-yellow cabinets and hunter green appliances. Everything in its place. Solei had to keep herself from scoffing. *Always so perfect, Mother. Except when you're not.*

Solei turned her gaze toward the small grove of trees that had sprung up from behind the white fence before she felt Luz staring at her. Their eyes met, but Solei looked away.

A part of her felt sorry for her mother—the perfect homemaker and wife who tried to control every outcome of her life, but couldn't stop her husband from cheating. Besides doing things the "proper" way, trust, loyalty, and family were everything to Luz. Solei worked to push down the deep resentment that she felt for her dad.

Luz broke the silence. "Earth to my daughter. Are you ready to get started? You can't bring your tea into the office— the papers are much too important."

Solei nodded and made a show of putting her teacup into the sink. She wanted Luz to make her clean it and her mother took the bait. Luz gave her daughter *the look*—eyebrows raised, eyes wider than usual, and pursed lips.

"I know, Mama. I'm going to run to the bathroom really quick. Where's Papi?" she asked no one, as Luz had already disappeared through the foyer to the office. Solei rushed over and peeked her head through the cracked door. "Where's Papi?" she asked again.

"Not here, obviously," said Luz. She sighed, long and loud, before replying, "He is out of town for a few days— business. Should be in by…"

Before Luz could finish her sentence, Solei had already made her way upstairs, looking, as she always did, at the family photos that lined the ascending wall. She scrutinized each framed moment, looking for evidence of an unfaithful father, and while she could find none, the pictures somehow felt emptier. She wondered if her newly discovered half-sister had family photos of smiling faces and people who loved her and gave her the world. What would her life have been like without her father, Alberto?

Solei pushed into her parents' bedroom, cringing with a fleeting sense of ickiness. "Alright Papi, where would you hide a secret photo?" She knew her father well enough to know he would keep it in the bedroom. Solei eyed the mahogany nightstands and Tiffany lamps beside the immaculate bedding. A chuckle escaped at the sight of the serape quilt, folded at the foot of the bed.

Any hint of their Peruvian heritage was her father's doing. Her mother decided that a life of prominence and wealth, especially in the Back Mountain, was synonymous with culture-free décor. This mindset began slowly after Solei overheard one of her mother's "friends" mention how "ethnic" the décor was.

Not the bookshelf. Solei knew her mother read those. It had to be his nightstand. Solei rummaged through the drawers, which mostly consisted of socks and sample toiletries, but then something sliced her fingertip. She pulled out a little black book. Fearing her mother might come looking for her, she pocketed the passport-sized notebook and quietly left the room.

***

"That doesn't go there," Luz barked, snatching the paper from Solei's hand as she tried to add it to a blue folder.

Together they had decided on a color-coded system, but Solei's decisions were met with Luz's snatching and sighing.

"Mama, that was a bank statement. Finances go in the blue folders, right?" Solei asked for what felt like the fifth time. Fighting the urge to scratch at her palms, her jaw tightened and her teeth clenched together. Before her mother could answer or respond with a dirty look, Solei huffed and sat down. She hoped her mother was as done with this process as she was. She stared at her mother, unblinking, sighing aloud again before she stood to straighten more folders.

After another hour of snatching, sighing, and bickering, Luz threw up her hands, "*Ay mi hija,*" signaling that she was done with this venture.

She made a show of tidying up while Solei studied the crow's feet at the corners of her eyes. She was still a formidable beauty, simply weathered by the life of a Hispanic woman.

Solei loved her dearly, feeling both anger and sorrow at what her mother endured at her father's hands. Part of her didn't want to face her parents and their lies, but another part—a part she could not ignore—wanted to throw their imperfections back in their faces. After years of feeling like they silently—and many times, not so silently—insisted she be perfect, like she had to say and do all the right things at all times, Solei wanted answers—and maybe to hurt them, just a tiny bit.

"Mama, let's get together for dinner—you, Papi, and I. I miss your home-cooked meals," Solei admitted, the truth slightly bent.

"This weekend?" Luz asked, a broad smile unfolding across her face. If Luz missed her daughter, it was evident solely in the long sighs and complaints about her "never" coming around.

"Yes," Solei replied, returning a cheeky smile. "I'll be here at four on Saturday?"

***

On the way back to her place, Solei scratched furiously at her palms at every stoplight and sign. She grappled with excitement and fear at the thought of confronting her parents. She rehearsed the quips and passive-aggressive remarks she could make at dinner before launching into their craziness.

Complaining and arguing with them were never allowed, but it was now fair game. Solei needed to practice her approach: the heat of the moment wasn't quite right. Respect was big in her household—though her mother never did show much respect to her father behind closed doors.

Solei was now an adult… and her parents had been lying and cheating and generally doing terrible things. This was the one and only chance she would ever have to freely speak her mind.

"Hey Google, call Camila Bestie." Solei prayed she would answer.

"*Hola, mi amiga,*" Camila answered, winded.

"*¿Qué te pasa a ti?* Why are you out of breath?" Solei asked.

"Running. What's up?" Camila replied.

"It's on. This Saturday at 4 p.m. Please tell me you can come," Solei pleaded. She didn't think she could face her parents alone.

"I don't know about that. This is a private family thing," Camila said between breaths. "Besides, I have a client on Saturday."

"You know my mom starts dinner early. What time is your client? You can meet me at my parents'."

"Fine. I need to finish this run," Camila said. "Besides, I know if I don't hang up soon, you'll just keep going."

***

Satisfied, Solei pulled up to her two-bedroom townhouse in Luzerne—the middle of three cramped together on the desolate Pennsylvania road. The home was a dirt-white structure with gutters overflowing with leaves, remnants of birds' nests and excrement. The makeshift porch, having an unstained staircase to the door, was in sharp contrast to the house. It was the only one on the block without a driveway.

Solei had cringed when she first saw the place, but at the time, she needed to get away from Luz, and focused instead on the interior photos she saw online. Its saving grace was the updated interior and spacious backyard of trees. Crossing the threshold was like being transported into a new land through a magic wardrobe. The living room's faux-wood floors were a beautiful dark gray. It was small, but clean with newly carpeted stairs that led to the second floor—no hallway, just one decent-sized bedroom to the left and the other to the right. She used one as an office-slash-yoga studio and the other for her bedroom. Both walk-in closets were occupied with her expansive collection of clothing and shoes.

With all that was going on with her parents, she could breathe freely here. It wasn't much, but the place was hers—hers to decorate and retreat to.

The book. Solei still wasn't quite sure she should read it—not for any sense of invading her father's privacy—but because she was afraid of what other secrets she might uncover.

She decided to have a bite before delving in. Before heading into the kitchen, she tossed the tote with the book onto her antique sofa—she couldn't be without *all* her usual luxuries. Smoked salmon and pasta were on the menu. Then, having no other beverage options, she poured herself a large cup of Moscato.

Within a few bites of her dinner, Solei reclined with one arm hoisted up on the sofa, tapping her fingers on the wine glass. "It's now or never." She reached into her tote and pulled out the little black notebook.

The diary contained the year's monthly calendars on the first pages and grid paper throughout the rest. Solei skimmed the calendars first, starting from the beginning of the year. The scribblings seemed to be in code; the boxes were too small for the words, but her eyes landed on two words that jolted her heart: *We met!*

She wanted to burn the book, but maybe she was jumping to conclusions. Yet almost every week after that entry, the words *"Hija Time"* appeared in the small boxes. Solei's throat tightened as she thought back to each instance—none of them were spent with her. She snapped the book shut and doubled over, dry heaving into a nearby garbage pail.

Chapter 5

Luz

"**M**i amor, I'm going to be home late tonight, but I *will* be home. If you can, wait up for me. I want to talk," Alberto said in the voicemail.

The message concluded with a beep and Luz turned to stare into the kitchen. She stood still, though her mind was racing. She hated cooking for one and... she didn't want to hear what Alberto had to say. The last time he used those words, there was an affair. She shuddered as her left hand moved to scrape against her right palm.

Slowly, Luz moved through the sala. *I've built a good life, haven't I?* She fluffed the pillows of the sofa, then folded and refolded the seldom-used throw. The wax warmer on the television stand pumped the room with the smell of daffodils. Luz took in two rapid breaths, becoming light-headed. She stumbled toward the kitchen to make a list for Saturday's dinner with Solei.

For just a second, she thought of River, a name she hadn't heard in some time. Luz's stomach tightened as her body remembered—the porch light that lit the threshold and River standing with wet eyes.

"Oh. I'm sorry… well, you may as well hear this, too," River had said, stifling tears. She looked down and rubbed her belly pensively, then yelled into the small foyer. "Alberto, where are you?"

"Don't yell into my home," Luz told her. She almost missed it—the small bulge under River's white, flowing maxi dress. She recalled the bile that rose in her throat, how she wanted to slap the woman, drag her inside if only to avoid the eyes of neighbors. Instead, she took a step back, slammed the door in River's face, then scrambled through the house, looking for Xanax and her senses.

"*Oye, cabrona,* you don't get my husband—my family," Luz had said to no one. She yanked the junk drawer open, scrambling to find the envelope of Xanax, and after contemplating taking several, she chose only one.

Luz remembered the bang at the door; she shrieked in anger, not sure what to do. It wasn't enough that the woman had intruded upon her marriage, but she thought she could just show up whenever she wanted—and with child! Luz stood for a few seconds with her eyes closed, wishing that the memory was a nightmare. The banging. *The neighbors will see,* she had thought, burning with rage. Then she spotted her checkbook on the counter.

She sped to the door as her hands moved furiously over the check. She opened the door and shoved the check into River's face. "Take this and don't ever come back!" she demanded, glancing to the left and right, conscious of the neighbors before slamming the door.

She stumbled up the stairs, thinking about the tearful woman clutching her protruding stomach. She hadn't taken off her clothes or put them in the color-coded laundry bins; she hadn't taken off her makeup or washed her face. Luz didn't shower and moisturize; she didn't change into her sleepwear or make Alberto's tea. That night, she collapsed onto their bed—house shoes and all—and the next morning she woke up early enough to make Alberto's breakfast.

Luz shook off the memory as if it were lice. "*Arroz, gandules...*" Thinking aloud, she pulled a chunk of the notepad off the refrigerator. She walked into the pantry, a source of her pride. Every spice and staple sat, perfectly decanted into clear jars, properly labeled, and sealed with white vacuum tops. Even the chestnut shelves were labeled so that everything could be put back exactly where they belonged. Alberto built the shelves to her exact specifications. Aside from his one indiscretion, he was a good man. At every twinge of rage, she considered the little things—the things he'd built or fixed around the house, how he had loved and provided for her and Solei.

"You're a good man, Alberto," she said aloud.

Her best medicinal friend would provide a good night's sleep before they had a talk. Luz instead busied herself shopping for the weekend meals. She cleaned their already spotless home, read on the wraparound porch, and laid out her clothes for the next day. At exactly 9 p.m., she checked all of the locks, brushed her teeth, moisturized, and slipped underneath her duvet.

Alberto

A few hours into the night, Alberto cracked open the bedroom door. "*Mi amor,*" Alberto whispered.

When Luz didn't budge, he walked with socked feet to the master bathroom and looked in the mirror. The stress of the last few weeks showed in his eye bags. After washing his face and hands, he dried them on the towel near the his-and-her sinks, then climbed into bed and wrapped his arm around his wife.

"Luz, you awake?"

Her breath hitched, but she didn't stir.

"*Te amo*" he whispered before rolling over to see a piping-hot cup of tea.

Alberto played out the conversation he would have with Luz. He decided to rise and find his agenda to jot his thoughts, but when he couldn't find it, he ventured into his office where he sat to write on a single piece of paper.

Why should he feel sorry for wanting to know his child? Why wasn't it on Luz to apologize—to understand what this need was all about?

***

The next day, Alberto felt a bit raw—no longer scared of hurting Luz. As usual, he awoke to Luz's empty side of the bed and the smell of fried salami. Thoughts of the last few months came flooding in, so Alberto took his time before he approached the needed conversation with Luz.

"*Cariño*, are you still in that bed?" Luz called to him.

Get out of bed, hombre, you have places to be, he told himself.

Under the pretense of stretching and getting ready, he took a few more minutes to head downstairs. Looking at himself one last time in the mirror, beads of sweat dotted his forehead. Although he wore the usual suit style, he fidgeted and wondered what *she* would think of it.

Luz smiled pleasantly as Alberto descended the stairs. She reached to grab his plate and mug, her cardigan whipping upward. Her linen pants had the perfect amount of loose and snug, her chest sat perky and poised under her sweater.

He appreciated her strength and confidence. Since his affair, however, a little bit of each was gone—not quite enough to keep her from putting on an air of confidence, but enough that he knew the confidence with which she now moved was a partial façade.

Luz placed the crockery on the island, motioning for him to sit. He could see intensity in her eyes. As they sat and sipped their tea, both avoided eye contact.

Finally, Luz said, "just tell me."

Alberto swallowed hard. "I know, Luz," he blurted. "I know about her—mine and River's daughter."

Luz appeared nauseous, pulling her mug from her face.

Alberto feared she might throw it at him.

Instead, she delicately placed the teacup upon its saucer, lowering her hands out of sight. She silently stared at him.

"Well?" Alberto said. "Nothing to say? That would be the first—"

Luz interrupted. "What the hell is there to say? You cheated, Berto, and didn't even have the decency to protect yourself or this family." Her ears grew red before she took a deep breath.

"So, you're not even going to apologize? Right." Alberto said. "Well, we've met, her and I. We've *been* meeting. Her name is Marigold, and she's smart and conscientious. She has two jobs—she pursues her real passion in library science as a library assistant and works part-time in a café to help pay her way through college—"

Luz interrupted him again. "What exactly is the point of this conversation? You've met her—great for you. Now, what? You want to pay for her college? Going to invite her to family dinners now?"

She gave him an exasperated look. She was angrily scraping her palms again. She picked up the teacup, took a slow sip. She looked out the window for a moment, then squared herself.

"*Calmate.* I haven't even told her who I am yet. As far as she knows, we're friends," Alberto continued. "I thought we could have a civilized conversation about this. I thought we could discuss everything, so that it would feel right... better... to tell her who I am."

"Over your dead body," Luz hissed before she slammed and shattered the teacup.

Chapter 6

Marigold

The anticipation of his return—the big announcement—caused her to rethink everything. She tried not to let the bad thoughts flood in and become a tsunami. The lack of communication enraged her, causing her to hate herself. *Why?* Why did she touch his arm that night? Why did it seem to bother him? Who had Alberto seen?

She recalled their meeting at *Tea, Read, Love* toward the end of her shift. He seemed a little in his head as they sat at the small round-top.

She made sure to reveal her legs as she'd been told they were one of her better features. Alberto, on the other hand, didn't seem to notice them dangling from the high-backed chairs.

The two sat in the corner, just out of sight of the large café window. It was romantic, and she hoped for a little physicality to feel wanted—sexually.

Alberto's eyes slowly traveled down to her hand as she laid it on his arm. Suddenly, he looked past her, his eyes widening. *Maybe his wife or daughter is behind us?* she thought.

She didn't dare turn around. Instead, she withdrew her hand and spent the rest of their time trying to meet his gaze.

It wasn't until days later that he told her about the business trip. She spent the next few days overanalyzing all their interactions, beginning to hate herself, and she hated him for making her fall so deeply. Instead of popping one of her prescribed sleeping pills, she decided to pop three.

Chapter 7

Camila

Camila's eyes swept the room until they landed on a young woman by the far window who looked as though she would break down. After locking eyes for a second, Camila quickly turned her head.

She ordered the iced coffee on special and found a table with her back to the crying girl.

As a student of psychology, Camila often found herself eavesdropping or, better put, people-watching. It never hurt anyone and it made her a better counselor—or so she told herself. Hours were spent observing passersby, trying to intuit what their lives were like. It was totally normal. And this time, she had a vested interest in surveilling this woman.

Wasn't crazy ol' Berto in here with you a few days back? Camila thought to herself, sipping her latte.

A few sips in, the woman placed a call. "Alberto, where are you? You've been gone all… *ugh,* just call me back and let me know what's going on."

She pondered the events and how they fit together. Alberto had been the source of pain for those around him since Solei was a little girl. When would it stop? Another one of his victims sat behind her, tapping away at her phone, no doubt sending a furious text to *good ol' Berto.*

Camila fought the urge to turn around and confront the woman. *What are you doing with my best friend's father?*

Before Camila could make up her mind about the possible explanations, there was a soft screech from the chair behind her. The downtrodden woman slowly walked past her, and Camila knew what she had to do.

She got up—too fast—spilling whipped cream on the table and floor. Navigating through the café, she tried to catch up with the young woman.

"Excuse me," she called as she neared the bathroom. Camila instantly regretted approaching when she turned around. "Are you here to meet Alberto Quispe?"

"Who are you?" The woman asked, her eyes flooding with tears.

"Just don't… okay. I know he's who you came to see. He's not who you think he is."

"Are you… are you his daughter?"

"It doesn't matter. Just ask him. Ask him to tell you who he *really* is," Camila said before turning away.

Alberto

For several seconds, no one moved at the sound of the shattering teacup. Luz's eyes burned into Alberto's as though to say, "Do what I say—or else."

He sat, absorbing her wrath until she finally relented and moved toward the pantry to fetch the broom and dustpan.

Alberto didn't dare move. He hated himself for his fear, but he knew better than to push his wife. Luz had never physically hurt him, but her psychological tactics made him wish she had. She always knew what to say—what calculated move could make someone suffer. So he sat there, waiting—not knowing for what, exactly.

Luz slowly swept the pieces from the counter into an empty container. "*Levantarse*," she snarled.

Alberto obediently stood, taking one last look into her eyes before rushing toward the door. He had to get away. The words "over your dead body" unnerved him.

He locked himself inside his Lexus before closing his eyes and taking a deep breath. Once he gained composure, he pulled off, seeing Luz standing in the doorway with an eerie smile.

He still had to meet Marigold soon, but his wife's threat gave him pause. Marigold deserved to hear the truth, and he knew that, but what would Luz do? She was typically one step ahead of him in everything. She had to know that he knew about his long-lost daughter, but maybe she did not know that they were meeting regularly.

Something inside him churned. Yes, he had cheated and hurt his wife, but wasn't turning River away the retribution?

The car moved faster with his rising anger. His foot weighed heavier and heavier on the gas pedal. He understood Luz not wanting to let River break up their marriage, but hadn't he chosen her after all? Or had he really chosen Solei? Alberto couldn't tell anymore, but he knew one thing—as fierce as Luz was for the perfect nuclear family, he would be for his children.

The other lanes and cars were a blur as Alberto sped over the Cross Valley, his focus on his final destination.

"Fuck you! Fuck it all to hell!" he yelled at the top of his lungs. He saw the exit ahead and punched toward it.

Flashing reds and blues broke him out of his trance. His rage flattened as he pulled onto the shoulder, reaching automatically for his license and registration. For a split second, he thought he saw Luz, but there was no one else besides the officer and a hefty ticket that awaited him. Afterwards, he texted an apology that he was running late.

When he finally arrived, he felt relieved. He looked through the café window, seeing Marigold anxiously clasping a drink between her hands.

He gathered his keys—and nerve—and reached for his wallet from the passenger seat. That's when he saw a reflection staring back at him in the café window. He squeezed his eyes shut, concerned he may finally have lost his mind, but when he opened them, Luz was there. She sat in her own Lexus across the narrow street.

Run, something inside him whispered, but he shook off the thought.

"You're being ridiculous, Alberto," he said aloud. He turned his head to face straight, trying to get a look at her without facing her head on. He hadn't remembered being this scared of Luz—not for years—not since he confessed the affair.

"Hi Mr. Quispe," a cheerful voice beckoned. As he looked up, a small yelp escaped at the sight of Camila standing on the sidewalk adjacent to the café window.

"Oh no, I scared you," she said. "Grabbing a bite?"

Alberto cleared his throat, looked across the street at the empty spot, and croaked, "Um, nope. Just leaving. But great to see you." And before Camila could reply, he peeled out so fast that his tires burned rubber on the road.

Sweat gathered on his forehead as he drove, looking for a place to pull over. Finally, he pulled onto a back road near Wilkes-Barre General Hospital.

He took a few deep breaths and pushed his fingers into his temples. His phone shrilled through his car's Bluetooth, making him jump.

Solei's name flashed onto the radio screen. She had been calling him all week, but he kept telling himself he would call her back… after he told Marigold the truth. One day after another passed, and before he knew it, too much time had passed for it not to be awkward when he admitted who he was. Solei had had her entire life with him. Marigold needed him now; she needed the truth.

For a second, Alberto struggled to breathe; his chest and face tightened. He stepped out of the car and into the open air. Seconds later, he looked up to see a car bumper barreling toward him.

Chapter 8

Marigold

Marigold's tormented scream echoed off the foyer walls of her house. The sound was matched by the rattling of the windows when she slammed the front door. Her face burned; sweat beading as her breathing raced.

She looked at her upturned palms, squeezed her hands into a fist, then swept her arm across the console table. The small basket, picture frame, and plant crashed to the floor. Glass crunched under her feet as she moved through the foyer, past her living room and bedroom, and toward the kitchen.

"Mother-effer!" she yelled into the air. "When. Is. It. My. Turn?" she continued between the slamming of every dish and utensil of her blood-red place settings.

Her table was always set for four, although she never had company. Marigold turned toward the counter, looking for the knife block, but spied the half-empty wine glass. She gulped down the last of it, wiped her mouth and tears with one motion, then whispered to herself. "How stupid can you be?"

After refilling the glass—with red instead of white this time—she sulked to the foyer to grab her purse from the floor, then burst through her bedroom door. The heap of clothing sat on the bed—the fanfare of choosing the perfect outfit. Marigold whipped the clothing off her bed so hard that it landed in a pile in the hall.

She shoved her fingers through her hair, squeezing until her knuckles turned white. Then, something clicked.

After checking her purse first, she stomped out of the house.

As she climbed into her car, Marigold voice-called her psychiatrist's office.

"I can't take it anymore. I'm tired of the games. Why do men always do this? No more! He's going to decide now or else," she yelled. That wasn't the message she intended to leave.

***

When Marigold returned home and put the key in the lock, the door popped open. There was no room in her mind to speculate. Marigold was sweating profusely now. She looked at her hands and they were trembling. She looked at the mess she didn't remember making. Her eyes burned, but no tears came. Marigold squeezed her fists into her temples as hard as she could, trying to shut out the screaming in her head.

Her phone buzzed. She was too scared to answer, so she let the sound fade into the background. In a trance, she stepped over the mess, the clothing heap in the hall, and landed on her bed.

Without hesitating, she tossed too many pills into her mouth and swallowed them with a long sip of wine, then crawled under her duvet.

Chapter 9

The Next Day

Solei

The clock read 3:12 p.m. "Dammit," Solei whispered. She sat there in the *sala*, sweating, anger swelling because Camila was late yet again. This time it mattered.

Solei wanted to confront her parents about the lies but couldn't do it alone. In truth, she was more anxious about Camila not accompanying her than she was about being late. Camila was *always* late. Solei glared at the clock—willing time to slow. *I'm supposed to meet my parents in thirty minutes.*

Today, Solei cursed her parents' choice to live in the wilderness-filled corner of Dallas, Pennsylvania that she'd always loved so much. Instead of practicing her speech, she paced the room. The sky-blue walls were supposed to be calming—at least that's what the guy at Home Depot told her. Instead, the blue made her feel trapped, like she was drowning in a façade of a happy life.

Where are you? Solei mouthed the words as her phone buzzed. Taking a deep breath, she answered, "*Coño*, girl, I thought you were almost here."

Camila sounded out of breath and started to tell Solei something, but the words came like a stream of consciousness. Solei couldn't focus, so she feigned interest but couldn't indulge her best friend too much, or else she'd certainly be going to see her parents alone.

Exit 2, okay—she's on her way.

Blaring horns and full-force winds sounded over the Bluetooth, snapping Solei out of her growing wave of anxiety.

"Hello?" Solei replied, "I hate it when you call me from the car… What? No, I don't want you to call me back…"

At this moment, another car honked on the other end of the line; its incessant cry became a whisper compared to the deafening sounds that followed. *Pop. Crunch.* Then Camila's clipped, muffled scream.

Chapter 10

Camila

reathe. Camila gasped; all she could do was breathe. Sight blackened. Heart racing. The sound of breath roared through her lungs and chest.

What's happening? Her eyes opened, but the swift transport from the ambulance to the emergency room was white and fuzzy.

The light bulbs above passed as though on a speeding conveyor belt. Someone in the background barked orders. Meanwhile, Camila's mind flashed to a movie montage of an ER lobby.

"The hospital," she whispered. "Solei..."

She was soon hushed while hands and arms appeared and disappeared over and across her body like a zoetrope. As her vision faded and expanded, she began to wish for the black whenever it materialized, then she faded into its deep, dark void.

"Camila, honey, *es tu madre*," a familiar voice said. "Your cousin's *quince* is in two weeks. You need to get up."

"I think… I think they'll understand," Camila tried to say, half smiling, although it felt as if sand was in her mouth. A hoarse whisper of a sound was all that eked out. Her mom's face, and the room, were blurred, but Camila could imagine the worry lines on her mother's forehead, and how wide her eyes must have been when she yelled for the nurse.

And just like that—more hands, and blurry faces. Camila wiped her eyes as she saw her father tightly holding her mother as she cried dramatically in the corner. *Shouldn't I be the one getting comforted?*

After much fanfare and time, the doctor entered to give Camila the prognosis. She had a broken nose, a few cuts and bruises, a concussion, and two broken ribs, but was otherwise okay. The airbag had done more damage than the crash.

Her mother, Anna, sat, teary-eyed, in a chair next to the bed, holding Camila's hand. She held on much too tight, but Camila didn't dare pull away. Her mother only let go periodically, with one hand at a time, to wipe her sweaty palms on her blue jeans; her white blouse stained with tears and makeup. Despite the doctor's reassurances, the fear seemed engraved into her mother's fine lines along with a long life of worry.

"Solei is downstairs grabbing coffee," she said. "When she called us and then we heard about the accident on the Cross Valley, *Dios mío*, I started calling every hospital. You scared me, *mija*."

"I'm fine, Mama," Camila said, too exhausted to console her mother.

Solei

Solei paced the hospital café waiting for her order. The sterile white walls and gray tables made her think of her mother. *Bland.* She waited, watching diners push tables together to accommodate their groups before settling in to sit and talk. She tried her dad again, getting his voicemail. *Where are you, Dad?*

Solei snapped back into the present at the call of her name and managed a smile for the cashier in the cash exchange for a coffee and bagel.

Walking back to the hospital room, the tray vibrated in Solei's hands. The fluorescent lights and gray floors reminded her of vomit. Her palms began to sweat when she saw the doctor emerge from Camila's hospital room. She pushed through the door, thinking the worst, but was surprised to see Camila awake and talking.

"I'm okay, Ma," Camila said, almost yelling. Coverage of the accident flashed across the TV screen. "Dad, pass me the remote!"

"...What was thought to be just another accident on the Cross Valley today is now being investigated..." the reporter on the television said.

"C'mon, *mija*, I don't know if I can watch this—" Camila's mom began.

The reporter continued, "...witness statements indicate fault with the driver of a red 2003 Jetta. Police are asking any other witnesses to contact them."

Images of a driver being taken from the scene in an ambulance flashed across the screen.

At this, Camila sat up straight, wincing as though from pain. "That's her! That's the crazy lady I was telling you about," she said.

Lumps of bagel dropped out of Solei's mouth as Anna poured out a barrage of questions. She kept pushing Camila for answers, but Camila didn't recall much beyond the way the driver was acting.

"Ma, I am tired—and dizzy," she complained, "I think—I just need some space right now. Why don't you and dad go home to freshen up a bit?"

Camila's suggestion went unheard. Anna kept going with the questions.

"I think that a little bit of rest will help Camila remember things," Solei added, hoping the hint might help.

"*Mi amor,*" Manny started gently, "what do you think about a nice home-cooked meal para nuestra bebé?"

Anna never could turn down a chance to feed a loved one. She gathered her things, a hint of delight dulling the previous concern from her face. The two kissed their daughter on opposite sides of her face, and Anna looked back one last time before being pulled along.

Solei closed the door behind Camila's parents, turning back toward her best friend.

"Gotta love 'em, right?" Camila said with a weak grin. "By the way, I'm so sorry about your parents—and their whole… freaking novela."

"That's not important right now," Solei replied. "Although I don't know what's worse—that my father had an affair, or that my mom kept a sibling from him and me. You know, my dad hasn't even bothered to answer my calls."

"He hasn't?" Camila grew quiet, then spoke after a minute or so. "I really am sorry I was late, but also—kind of not. *This* may not have been an accident."

"Seriously?!" Solei asked.

"I mean—I wish I knew what the police knows." Camila said. "Can you stay with me for a few days? I want to get the hell out of here, but they won't let me go home alone with a concussion."

"Sure. I'll go and get the nurse," Solei suggested, exiting the room.

Solei returned with the nurse who was checking notes on a clipboard.

"So, Camila...," the nurse began, "the doctor would rather you stay a day or two longer, but if your sister promises to stay and keep a close eye for any signs of trouble, then we can discharge you."

Solei didn't correct the nurse's innocent mistake. She and Camila were merely best friends, but Solei again drifted into thoughts of her father's affair and the half-sister she had just learned about—along with all of her family's secrets and lies.

"… Earth to Solei," Camila said. The sound of Camila calling her name ratcheted Solei out of her thoughts. She turned to see her friend, wincing as the nurse pulled out her IV.

"I'm sorry? What did you say?" Solei asked.

"I said… can you text my parents and let them know that I'm being discharged, and that I'm staying at your place?"

"A sleepover?" Solei asked, working to hide her enthusiasm in a tone of surrender. "Fine."

***

In the car ride to Solei's apartment, Camila seemed to squirm in deep thought. With every pothole, she'd ask, "Do you think it was stupid to leave the hospital?"

Solei tried to reassure her. "I think being comfy, having good food and better company than the doctors is a better recipe for recovery," Solei suggested. "Anyway, how's the studying and internship going?"

"Honestly, I think I'm ready for this exam," Camila replied. "I just want to get it over with already; it can take almost 90 days to get the license in the damn mail? That's assuming I pass. Why did I decide to become a Licensed Professional Counselor again?"

"For the same reason you got a bachelor's degree in criminal justice. Something about making a difference in the prison system, *yada yada*." Solei scoffed. "Have you gotten to practice with inmates yet?"

"Pretty sure I'm not supposed to tell you if I did," Camila laughed. "I've observed and studied case notes, but I spend most of my internship time in a general counseling office. I can't really treat anyone until I am licensed. What about you, Miss World-Renowned Curator?" Camila asked.

"It's Miss Regular Associate Curator." Solei laughed bitterly. "You know you're either world-renowned or you're no one to my mother."

Both women sighed heavily. Silence loomed, then lingered, provoking their eyes to the autumn outside of their individual windows.

Chapter 11

Solei

The sunlight flickered on Solei's eyelids. She stretched as she counted down from five, then checked off the list—*not enough sleep, breakfast, dive back into Dad's agenda*. Tears threatened, and beads of sweat pooled at the back of her neck.

Before getting up from her bed, she looked down at her best friend—drooling, but otherwise looking better than the night before. Solei carefully unwrapped herself from the duvet so as not to disturb Camila.

After slipping on her socks, she made a beeline for the kitchen to make chamomile tea. She gazed out at the morning's light, stirring her tea bag and wondering why her father was ignoring her calls.

The agenda called out to her. The whole matter pulled emotions out of her she didn't know were there, deepening the divide between her and her father. She set her cup on the nightstand and carefully pulled the book out. After a glance toward Camila, Solei snuggled into the duvet and opened it.

The entries—*Hija Time*—stung like a thousand paper cuts. *Daughter Time?*

"What about me?" Solei scoffed. "Dad, where are you anyway? Call me back." She couldn't read on; she had spent years tamping down her emotions, and now they threatened to burst.

Camila stirred. Solei wished she could swap places with her. She quickly replaced the damned thing, then tried to reach her dad. Again.

"You've reached Alberto Quispe," the recording began, but Solei didn't want to leave another voicemail. Her father had been unreachable far more in the last few months than her entire life. Solei's stomach tightened. Just as something was bubbling up inside her, Camila had rolled over.

"Solei? *¿Qué te pasa?*" she asked, her eyebrows creased in a line.

"I just… my dad *still* hasn't called me back… and he isn't… answering *any* of my calls." Her voice cracked. "I just want my dad." She scratched at her already raw palm. "Sssh," she yelped as her nail caught on an existing split in her skin.

"Stop!" Camila demanded. She reached up and placed her hand under Solei's. Several thin reddish lines ran down the palm of Solei's hand, crisscrossing over with scabs and scars from older cuts.

Camila glared at her. "What the hell is this?! This is *not* a suitable way to express your emotions. Can we be real for a sec?"

Camila was familiar with abandonment—she was adopted with no contact with her biological parents. Her sudden silence finally coaxed a response from Solei.

"I don't know what else to say. You know what I am going through right now. I... I feel lonely, betrayed, like I want answers, but at the same time... finding out my mom is much worse than the literal worst I always thought she was—makes me feel relieved.

"I don't have to be her perfect daughter anymore. And for whatever reason, that makes me feel anxious, too. I guess in a way, it was my excuse to try and then fail... because I can blame my mom for putting too much pressure on me, even subconsciously, by being 'perfect' herself. At least her definition of perfect. Does that make sense?" Solei paused short of scratching at her palm. It was a relief to say it out loud, and to someone else. Camila wouldn't judge her and she knew that, yet she had fought this long not to say those words.

"That makes perfect sense. And it's okay to feel everything and to let it out, but *not* to hurt yourself. Therapy is great, but you have to find ways to cope that don't require another person. You hike, that's great. What about journaling?" Camila said.

Solei audibly scoffed. "Journaling, huh." She reached over, pulled out her father's agenda, then hesitated just for a second before shoving it at Camila. "Before you ask a million questions—it was my dad's. He... he met her... my sister."

"*Dios mío*, Solei. Why didn't you tell me that?" Camila said, looking back and forth between the book and Solei.

"I don't know." Solei said. She had handed out her father's private information. It felt like a betrayal.

When Camila didn't reach for the book, Solei replied, "Yeah, maybe that's too far."

She took the book back and placed it in her nightstand. "So far I've only found dates for a few of their meetings. It's harder than I thought to get through, mainly because he refers to *her* as his daughter. Those should have been *our* lunches and time. What about my mother? I'm so pissed… and sad… and…"

Solei's palms flew up to her face and squeezed into her temples, pushing until it felt as though blood vessels had burst under her eyes. As she let go, the grab in her chest loosened, and her breathing evened.

Camila looked back and forth between Solei and the bedroom door for several seconds.

"I'm sorry about that," Solei said, too calmly, as she smoothed her hair and clothing. A faint smile stretched her lips. "I'm hungry. You?"

Camila pursed her lips.

***

The two shuffled around the small kitchen, preparing their breakfast. Solei tried in vain to get Camila to sit and be waited upon, but she moved around the kitchen.

Neither seemed to want to discuss their individual situations, but sitting in silence seemed far from ideal. When the eggs and *salchicha huachana* were done, the two quietly stared at their plates. Both stood on either side of the high-top table, then looked up at each other and laughed.

"Alright, we need to watch something," Solei declared, moving from the table to the *sala*. "Not the news."

Camila parked on the couch while Solei pulled out the card tables. As they playfully debated over what to watch, the tension eased.

A television documentary played in the background as the women fell into their routine, chatting about less serious matters—their latest woes with dating, then the newest exhibition that Solei helped to curate. Their laughter rose like a war cry against all anxieties until a loud buzzing sounded from upstairs. The two yelped, exchanging a sullen look as Solei rose to see which one of them had been summoned by phone.

"Wait, let me," Camila interrupted.

"Uh, you're supposed to be resting, but… the bathroom *is* calling me." Solei turned up her nose, laughing as she hurried toward the bathroom. "It might be a long one."

Camila

Camila headed to the room searching until she spotted both phones—hers was flashing. She snatched it and quickly screened the notifications—work and school emails, three text messages, and a missed call from her mother.

Sighing, she knew she would have to call her mother back, and soon. Her mother was not beyond popping up at Solei's house.

"It's mine," she yelled toward the door before sitting on the side of the bed. She sent a quick text message to her mother to assuage her panic.

Then, she slowly pulled the nightstand drawer open, repeatedly looking over her shoulder. It was now or never. With the agenda in hand, she skimmed through the pages, finding entries about Marigold—*Hija Time*. Then, she looked for her own name.

Quietly, she tore out the pages where Alberto mentioned seeing her at Marigold's café. At the sound of Solei's toilet flushing, she gave the last page a quick and loud tug, coughing to mask the sound. For a second, she sat there looking at the pages.

"Now is not the time. There's still more to do," she said to herself. Camila yelled back down again. "It was my phone. I'll be down in a second."

She replaced the book and closed the drawer quietly.

She heard a sudden gasp from down the stairs. Camila jumped up and shoved the pages into her purse resting on the other side of the bed. She then rushed down to the living room with their phones in hand.

"What?!" Camila asked, wiping the sweat from her lip.

"She's a killer," Solei shrieked, sitting on the edge of the couch. Her eyes flitted back and forth on the screen.

Camila joined her, growing speechless at what they were hearing from the television.

"…The dead body of a Hispanic male in his early fifties was found in the trunk of a red Jetta involved in a recent accident. Police have detained the woman in connection with the body." A photograph of Marigold being taken from the scene in an ambulance flashed across the screen.

"The body." Camila cleared her throat. "…a body…in *her* trunk? I can't believe she…" Camila trailed off, her voice barely audible.

"Camila, you okay? Your face is white," Solei said, "Let's turn this off."

Camila shot up from the couch and charged upstairs to the bedroom. Frantically, she gathered her things and plopped on the edge of the bed so hard she almost slipped off.

"Camila! Camila!"

At the sound of Solei's beckoning, Camila trudged back downstairs.

"Camila, what is it? Are you… scared? You were nowhere near her in the accident, right?" Solei asked. "Say something. Why don't you take a nap, or we can put on one of those terrible novelas you love so much?"

Without a word, Camila stood up too fast, feeling as though she might break into a run, but instead sat back onto the sofa, closing her eyes. "I… I just need a nap," she finally said, heading slowly upstairs toward the bedroom. "I'm going to take a nap."

Solei nodded and obliged, watching her friend move slowly upstairs toward the bedroom. A few hours later, Solei awoke momentarily to the soft click of the front door before falling back to sleep.

Chapter 12

Detective Rose

"It wasn't an accident," Camila blurted when Detectives Rose and Hamilton entered the interview room. The two exchanged a confused look before Hamilton settled into her seat. Rose made a show of grabbing the other metal chair, flipping and straddling it.

"I'm sorry. What wasn't an accident?" Detective Rose asked, shifting his short, stocky wall of a body in irritation. He hated that they weren't able to start and steer the conversation. He didn't want conjecture or theories from this random "witness," and all they knew so far was that she claimed to have "helpful" information on the accident… not necessarily the body in the trunk.

Both detectives were already anxious that the media broke the story before they were able to speak to Marigold or even identify the body. It would color Camila's statement, and that of anyone else that came along. His partner, Detective

Hamilton—his opposite in appearance with her 6-foot stature, long nose, and olive skin—cleared her throat and gave him a look.

"I'm sorry, you all should start… it's just that… I saw that woman before the accident, and she was *loca*." Now she had their attention. Rose shifted in his seat as Hamilton began to talk.

"Go on," she said. Not interrupting an interviewee when they were bursting to talk was Interrogation 101.

Camila started to recount the events leading to the accident but was interrupted when she called the other driver Miriam. "Wait, I'm sorry… Miriam?" Hamilton checked her notes as though looking for that name.

"Not Miriam," Camila said with an embarrassed smile.

"Okay, look—" Rose began to say, but he was cut off by his partner.

"Why did you call her Miriam?" Hamilton asked.

"Sorry, I can get a bit animated sometimes. When I'm out and about, bored, I sometimes give strangers names, and fake lives. I'm… I'm a psychologist, so I play this speculative game with myself and strangers… as a way to avoid biases with actual clients. Basically, I decided she looked like a Miriam. Anyway… what is her name?" Camila asked.

The detectives shared another look.

Camila fidgeted in her seat. "Well, I saw on the news that you were looking for information. What kind of information were you seeking?" she probed.

"Due to the circumstances, we're not disclosing her name at this time. We were simply looking for information leading to the accident," Hamilton said. "We were hoping you could tell us which direction she came from, if there was anyone else in the vehicle with her, or any other details like that."

Rose stood again, no doubt wanting to switch focus.

"Can I start from the beginning?" Camila closed her eyes for a second, as though recounting the accident. "I stole a few looks at the woman at the red light; I tried not to stare. She was banging her fists on the steering wheel so wildly that her hair was thrashing across her face.

"Anyway, her face was covered in tears and makeup as though she was sobbing, but an incoming text message made me jump—it was my mom telling me not to answer while driving.

"Anyway, the woman in the red Jetta seemed to reach into her purse, and I had hit the gas not more than three seconds after the light turned green, and she honked obnoxiously, but cut *me* off, almost hitting my car.

"I was following in the same direction of her car, but heading toward Solei's parents' home. I was late so I called Solei over my phone's Bluetooth.

"The woman seemed to be having a mental episode. She was texting, barely avoiding collision with every car that merged from each exit. Her car then swerved into the left lane.

"That's when Solei answered, I told her I had to call her back, and as I hung up, the lady swerved toward yet another car. She looked over at me before slamming on the brakes.

"Before I knew it, we were all crashing. The airbag exploded in my face. There must have been glass flying: it was like a thousand paper cuts at the top of my head. Then it was over, or so I thought, but the lady stumbled out of her car.

Blood was pouring from the top of her head. I could hear her yelling and crying, 'I killed him' or maybe 'you killed him.' Anyway, the screams, the road, the cars, it all faded then."

When Camila finished her story, the room was silent. Rose took it all in as his partner scribbled rapid-fire notes.

"You believe the driver of the red car caused the accident?"

"I know she did," Camila said. "She slammed the brakes and almost crashed into me. If you can believe it, she wanted to crash—didn't matter with who."

"I believe you—just trying to discern the facts, and why you believe she caused the accident," Hamilton said.

"I'm trying to figure out why someone with a body in the trunk of their car would purposely cause an accident?" Rose blurted out.

"I told you. She was out of her mind. Anyway, that was my experience. Do with it what you will." Camila said. "But she saw my face. So, I wonder if I'm in danger here?"

Danger, really? Rose thought, but instead said, "You're safe."

"Thank you for stopping by, Miss Sanchez. You've been a big help today. Let me show you out. Here's my card. If you think of anything else, please give us a call," Hamilton said.

She waved as Camila moved towards the parking lot, but stopped on the precinct steps, pulling out her phone. Hamilton paused for a second, watching her closely, before reentering.

"What the hell was that?" she asked Rose.

"I know," he replied.

"I mean it was a good question, but just maybe not the

right time to ask it. Anyway, why would she intentionally cause the accident with a body in her trunk?" Hamilton asked, her eyebrows drawn toward one another.

"Benny, the woman is crazy. She probably didn't mean to hit the brakes, and so hard," Rose retorted. "Dammit! If these doctors don't wake her up, I will."

"And what do you make of this Camila person? It wasn't just me. That was weird. She comes in to give a perfectly crafted statement *and* kept trying to get information from us. It just doesn't sit right with me," Hamilton said.

"Everyone wants to be the one to crack the case, but yeah—no, something was definitely off there. We'll circle back to her. Let's check on this autopsy report," Rose replied.

Chapter 13

Camila

Camila sat in the Uber on the way back to Solei's, pissed off. She didn't feel that they took her seriously. Camila's mind buzzed as a plan formed. They had to believe her—it was imperative—but she couldn't tell them the real reason. She couldn't tell them about the woman in the red car and the café without giving away that she, too, was one of the last people to have seen Alberto alive. Then again… there was Luz.

Camila debated telling Solei the truth. She had already kept quite a few things from her, but how could she explain why she had gone by herself… why she hadn't shared her entire experience. She had to figure it out soon because she was almost back at Solei's. She figured Solei had to have a million questions. The palm scratching and her newest emotionality… her friend was hanging on by a thread.

As she pulled up, Solei was coming out through the front door. *Damn it!*

"You okay? Where'd you go?" Solei asked.

"Don't be mad. I was lying there thinking about it all. The crash, the news story, you, and I just felt helpless. I needed to do something. So… I went to the police station to give some information. I had to do it alone. You're going through enough," Camila said.

"Oh," was all Solei said.

"I just told them what I saw. How erratically the woman was driving, how she had almost crashed into me before *it* all went down. Then, these *tontos* started acting like I was some criminal. Acting like they didn't believe me. It was all a waste of my time, I think… I just wanted to be helpful." Camila sighed.

"I don't think that's what it was. They were probably just doing that thing police do—you know, act puzzled and repeat what you say back to you to probe for more information," Solei ventured.

"Well, they should be probing *her*, the *loca* that caused a major accident and had a body in her *pinche* trunk," Camila said, visibly shaken. "*Ugh*, I think I'm just hangry."

"What's Luz making for dinner?" Solei asked.

Camila raised an eyebrow at her, and they both laughed.

Chapter 14

Solei

Solei and Camila stood on the front porch waiting for Luz to open the door. Usually the perfect hostess, Solei was confused at how long it took Luz to answer.

"Are you sure she's here?" Camila asked, sounding winded as the sun beat down on them. She looked as if she were about to pass out. "Don't you have a key to this place?"

"Grouchy much? *¿Qué te pasa a ti?* I forgot it, okay. And it's early Monday evening, of course she's here. No doubt making dinner. And that's why we're here. We'll eat up, then get right to it. They can't avoid me any longer—" Solei was interrupted by the front door flying open.

"*Mija,* what are you doing here?" Luz asked uncharacteristically.

Her hair was disheveled, and her face was bare of makeup. Luz did not wait for her daughter to answer, but turned, shuffling away in her fuzzy house slippers and matching silk pajama set and robe. Solei had never seen her mother without makeup and in pajamas—unless already in bed for the night. And she never took naps, let alone slept in. Nor did she answer *the door* in pajamas.

Solei and Camila exchanged a look.

Solei decided against her original thought to ambush Luz. "*¿Mamá, estás bien?*" she asked instead.

"Aye, I'm fine. I'm not perfect, you know," she replied.

Solei had to physically keep herself from scoffing.

"*¿Y Papá? ¿Dónde está?*" She would usually see him or hear him singing.

"Want some tea?" Luz asked, filling the tea kettle, while staring absent-mindedly out of the window. "*Y tú*, Camila? You look like hell. Why aren't you in the hospital?"

"*Estoy bien*. I would love some tea. Have anything for a headache?" Camila asked.

Luz reached into the white cabinet above the drying mat and pulled out three teacups and saucers. Then, she shuffled over to the refrigerator, but as she reached for the medicine basket, her hand simply lingered in the air. Solei noticed this stutter. This wasn't the first time. Something was definitely wrong with her mother.

Hamilton

The Homicide Department was abuzz with chatter, phone conversations, and the tapping of keys. Hamilton and Rose sat at their respective desks, engrossed in their work.

"Looks like the crime techs are good for something," Rose said. "Marigold Hunter may have removed her victim's wallet, but she forgot something else. They found a business card wrapped up in the duvet."

Hamilton chuckled at her partner's wide smirk. For someone who is pessimistic with just about everything else, the smallest of clues seemed to bring him great pleasure.

"Well, let's see if he's who the card says he is… Okay, we may have an ID! It's a perfume shop. Pretty fancy for a place where one makes their own perfume. Anyway, the name on the card is…" Hamilton paused, lifting the card closer to her face. "Alberto Quispe. He got a ticket, we got his address."

When Rose didn't so much as grunt, Hamilton looked up to see him staring at his computer. "Earth to Jack."

"Heard you, sorry," he said. "I was scrolling through Hunter's socials. There's basically nothing on here, except her wanting to be a librarian. Don't young people share their whole lives on social media anymore? It's all flowers and books, yada yada on here. Nothing really personal. Not one passionate word, post, GIF—nil. Does that seem odd to you?"

"Maybe she's an old soul," Hamilton said, chuckling. "Anyway, come 'ere. This look like our guy?" Hamilton asked.

"That's him. Welp, I wouldn't call it a lead, but it's something, at least. Let's go."

As Hamilton plugged in Quispe's address into her car's GPS, she noticed Rose making his signature face. "What is it? You still on the social media thing?"

He didn't say anything for a few seconds; his eyebrows screwed together and his tongue clicking. "When did the victim get a ticket? His body was found in Hunter's car on Saturday."

"Let's see. I think it was Friday," Hamilton said. "Oh. The M.E. put his time of death at around 72 hours ago. Besides our killer, the officer was likely the last person to see Quispe alive."

"That's what I was thinking," Rose said. "He may be able to speak to Quispe's state of mind, maybe even more if he was observant enough. What was he ticketed for?"

"Speeding," Hamilton replied, raising an eyebrow at her partner. "I wonder what—or who—he was running from." Her words hung in the air as they made their way to provide the death notification to the family of the deceased.

As open and shut as this case may have seemed, a motive was necessary to sway a jury. They had to find out how the two were involved. Marigold's being in a coma was both beneficial and harmful to the case. It meant a race against her mind's clock—gathering as much evidence as possible before she woke, while also needing her to be awake to charge her.

***

On the drive, the two stared into the scenery; the ride down Chase Road was lush with tree after tree, peppered with fall hues. Hamilton hoped the fall weather and pastoral scenes would mellow her partner from his usual abrasiveness. Typically, he was great on death notifications, but she knew the case got under his skin. It was annoying her as well.

As they pulled up to the Quispe home, Hamilton felt a twinge in her stomach.

They approached the door to see a young woman whose curious face crinkled as she opened it. "Can I help you?" she asked.

"Hi. I'm Detective Hamilton and this is my partner, Detective Rose."

"Oh... how'd you know Camila is here?" Solei asked.

"We're not... here to see Camila... Can we come in please?" Hamilton asked, stealing a glance at her partner as they stepped into the foyer.

Question after question plagued her mind. *Could it be a coincidence?* They were there to give a death notification of a dead body to the family who has ties with a witness? Hamilton couldn't quiet her mind; she couldn't figure out where to start, but knew she had to before Rose opened his mouth.

"He's dead!" Solei cried out as she heard the news. "Are you sure it's him? Don't we need to identify the body?" The mother stood frozen. "Ma, don't just stand there. Say something. Ask something." Solei demanded. "How long? How long has he been gone? How did he die? Where was he?" The questions came out in rapid succession until they were only strangled yelps.

Rose's eyes cut toward Camila like daggers.

"It wasn't... he wasn't... not in that trunk?" Solei squealed.

Luz sat up at this revelation, but before she could speak, Rose interrupted.

"Can we please speak to you alone, Mrs. Quispe?" he said.

"Absolutely not. Just explain what it is that everyone seems to have figured out," Luz demanded.

"I'm sorry. Your husband—" Hamilton said, then turned to Solei, "and father... was found at the scene of an accident. We're exploring all the possibilities at the moment, but we're investigating it as a suspicious death on account of the location of his body and his injuries. He was... found in the trunk of one of the cars involved. According to the medical examiner, his injuries are conclusive with a hit and run victim—he places the time of death somewhere between Friday night and yesterday morning. I know this can be a difficult time, but the earlier we can ask… certain questions, the better chance we have of finding justice for you all."

Hamilton paused to give the family time to take it all in. The next questions would be hard—for them to hear and for her to ask.

Luz nodded as Solei silently wept.

"Did your husband seem off the past few days—scared even?" Hamilton asked as she trod toward the harder questions. "Also, it's been a day or two. Where was he supposed to have been between his passing and now?"

Between sobs and large gulps of air, Solei looked to her mother. Luz hadn't offered any explanation before now.

She simply said, "He's an adult. I don't track his comings and goings. Not sure if you know this, but my husband is—or was—a businessman with a franchise."

Solei scoffed loudly.

Hamilton made note of Solei's reaction, and of Luz's focus—talking up her husband's business.

Rose's cheeks reddened. "Ma'am, I'm sorry to be frank, but do you have any reason to believe that your husband was having an affair? Do you know someone by the name of Marigold Hunter?"

As soon as the name rolled off of Rose's tongue, all three women gasped. At this, Rose and Hamilton exchanged glances. No one moved, and no one spoke a word. For several seconds, each person seemed to be taking in one another, discerning what the next best thing to say could be.

Hamilton cut her eyes sharply at Rose. She would have kicked him in the shin if they weren't standing in an immaculate living room.

The woman Camila seemed to be heavily sweating at this point. The wife just sat there, unmoved. She didn't demand answers or ask any more questions.

"Why are you looking at us, treating us like suspects?" Solei blurted out. "Ma," she barked, rolling her eyes. "Yes, my father had an affair—twenty-something years ago. Marigold is the product."

Rose's mouth dropped open, and his eyes darkened. Hamilton signaled him to let her speak. She took a beat to digest the new piece of information as the word *motive* seemed to linger between them. "Let's have a seat and start from the beginning. You said your father had another child."

"Marigold is the illegitimate child of Alberto and a past lover. They were meeting, but as far as I know, he hadn't told her who he was yet," Luz said matter-of-factly. Her eyes filled with tears.

"Mama, I think they've figured that much out," Solei said. "My father didn't know Marigold existed, because my mother turned *her* mother away.

"Recently, my father received a letter from Marigold's mother—you know, there's a daughter, blah blah. I guess my dad was meeting with her, getting to know her. I mean, that's really it.

"Did she kill my father?" Solei asked, eyes welling up again, but she didn't cry. Instead, she squeezed her hands into fists so tightly that her palms turned red.

"I see," Hamilton said, acknowledging Solei's admission. She gave her the space to continue, and looked over at Rose who was visibly stewing. Averting her eyes, Hamilton continued when Solei didn't. "And how do you know this? Did your father confide in you?"

Luz looked at her daughter. "Even in death, 'Berto," she whispered.

Hamilton made a note of Luz's wide-as-saucer pupils, the bags under her eyes, the sweat beading around her forehead. She thought to ask if the woman was okay, but Solei interrupted.

"I wish…" Solei replied, wistfully. "I haven't talked to my father in almost a week. Not since I found the letter."

"It would be very helpful to see the letter," Rose chimed. "It would be very useful for our investigation."

"I'd love to see that letter, too," Luz said to the bewilderment of everyone.

Solei's head snapped towards her mother.

"So, you didn't know about the letter? Was it not mailed here?" Hamilton asked. Something about the look on Solei's face told Hamilton that Luz was playing a role. She intercepted her husband's mistress once before, but maybe it was sent someplace the wife couldn't get to it.

"No such letter was mailed to my house," Luz asserted.

"I'd like to see my father," Solei said, her voice trembling.

"We can release the body for viewing soon. I know this is difficult, but we just have a few more questions."

"I… I need to lie down. I'm sorry… I just—" Luz started to say, nearly toppling over as Hamilton rose to catch her by the arm. Luz corrected herself, then exited the living room before either detective could protest.

Taking the long way to the steps, Luz headed straight for something, then peeked over her shoulder, catching Hamilton's gaze. Then, she disappeared upstairs.

Chapter 15

Rose

Rose and Hamilton exchanged a look. Rose had to keep himself from audibly scoffing. *What the hell was that?* he thought, praying he didn't say it out loud.

He felt his excitement building. Yes, there was the family to consider, but a new understanding emerged from this interaction. While Marigold seemed the obvious choice for the hit and run, he couldn't ignore the niggling feeling in his chest and the fact that two other people in the Quispe house had motives. He looked up at Hamilton to see if she felt it, too, then asked, "When exactly did you see your father last?"

"I haven't seen my father in a couple of weeks. And no, that isn't unusual," Solei replied. "He is often out of town for business. In fact, he recently went out of town—what was it—Monday? He was supposed to come back Friday, so the three, er, four of us could have dinner on Saturday."

"The four of you?" Rose asked with a raised eyebrow. If they had invited Marigold here for dinner, that would throw a wrench in most of the theories developing in his mind.

"My parents, Camila, and I," Solei replied, too quickly.

"Hmm. Well, we'll be in touch soon about the release of your father's… er… your father," Rose said. "Please do give us a call as soon as you find that letter, or if you think of anything else. It's very important." Rose stood up, reaching for his card when his partner wrapped her hands around Solei's. She gave Solei's hand a squeeze, offering her condolences, then let go, placing her card on the coffee table.

Solei

Solei felt miserable about the way the detectives ferreted around the sad and private parts of her family's lives. Her family's darkest parts were going to be put on display until this case was closed. The mounting tension threatened to consume her altogether. But she smiled and thanked the detectives for their diligence, allowing Hamilton to take her hand, promising to let them know if she thought of anything else.

She watched as the detectives walked silently back to their vehicle; Detective Rose gave a quick look over his shoulder. She closed the door with a soft click.

On her way back to the living room, she paused for a second to take a slow glance up the stairs. She sat down on the couch with a huff, unable to wrap her head around her mother's behavior… and lies. She had done her best to excuse it for the sake of the police, but she saw how Hamilton and Rose repeatedly looked at each other. Her mother not wanting to be a part of the conversation was odd, to say the least, especially after she lied blatantly about the letter. Solei couldn't remember if she told the police that she found the letter in her parents' home office.

Solei was underwhelmed with their progress, but she noticed something she was sure the detectives did as well. She noticed the glances between her mother and Camila.

The detectives had subtly asked each of them about their whereabouts last Friday. Solei had been at work, and both Camila and her mother had their stories, but something was off. Something in the way their eyes and bodies shifted—in the way they glanced at one another—just for a second, but Solei saw it. She felt like she was in a maze of betrayal, secrets, and lies. And what of the coincidence that her best friend happened to be in that car crash with Marigold, the person who not only murdered her father, but had thrown him in a trunk like a piece of luggage.

It bubbled and bubbled until finally... the house rang with the shrill release of her anxiety.

Chapter 16

Camila

Camila wished she could be like the Quispes—fierce when it counted and weak when warranted. When the detectives were at the Quispes', their alternating stares shook Camila. They seemed to probe for faults in her previous testimony and watch for any behavioral tic. More than once, Detective Rose mentioned how fateful it was that Camila was at the Quispe home while having been involved in the crash with Marigold. There was also a damning significance to omitting her interactions with both Alberto and Marigold on the day of his death and keeping it from Solei.

It was too late now—Camila couldn't tell anyone—not about seeing Alberto and Marigold—or Luz.

Camila flushed the toilet and walked over to the sink to splash the worry from her face. Her nausea held persistently, along with the pain in her head that struck like flashes of lightning. Still, she emerged from the bathroom with an empathetic smile for her friend.

Solei sat at the glass dining room table, forehead plastered to its edge while her arms hung down at her sides. Camila imagined Luz admonishing her daughter for the *porquería* she was getting on the beautiful table.

Luz didn't seem to be coming out of her room anytime soon. Solei had told Camila that the last time there was *trouble* with Alberto, Luz had not emerged from her room for a week. That's no doubt because Alberto wasn't around. What Camila remembered was that no matter how Luz was feeling—sick, tired, whatever—she always tended to Alberto's needs.

Camila moved to comfort Solei. "It's okay, you know? To be both sad and pissed off. He was your father, but he had also been dodging you to be with a woman who ended up killing him."

Solei just stared at her. Maybe Camila had gone too far.

"What was all the nervousness about?" Solei asked.

"What?" Camila replied. "I don't appreciate your tone. Marigold is the suspect, but the detectives were asking some pretty pointed questions."

When Solei didn't respond, however, Camila added, "Because they kept treating me like a suspect. I wasn't the one with your father's body in the trunk." Camila paused and took a deep breath. "I'm sorry, that was insensitive. But you were here. They kept saying Marigold is the suspect but asking us questions like we were involved. You should probably be talking to your mother. Was it me, or was she acting weird for someone who just found out her husband has passed?"

"I'm sorry. You're right. The police were treating us like suspects," Solei said. "Truth is—I get it. My mother and I may have just as much motive as Marigold. I'm just so… I don't know, sad… mad. I'm mad at my dad, as harsh as that sounds. I'm mad at my mother, at myself. I just… I don't know how to feel.

My father had been dodging me, and now he's gone, so I don't feel like I have the right to be mad at him. I also never got the chance to forgive him. And… God, I feel like I'm losing my damn mind."

"Solei, you're currently in distress—in shock, really. That is totally okay. You are okay. Let's take some time to help comfort you. Would you rather lie down or sit up?" Camila asked.

"Sit up, I guess," Solei replied.

"Okay. Sit up straight, shake your hands out. Now, let's try slow, small neck rolls. Okay, now close your eyes and take several slow, deep breaths. Let go of whatever you can with each exhale. Whatever you can't let go, remember that feelings are temporary. Focus on centering yourself. Now, take a few more deep breaths. When you're ready, open your eyes."

Solei opened her eyes. "So much of this isn't adding up. My mother's behavior, my father's behavior leading up to his death, this weird police investigation, and…" Her voice trailed off. "We have to get out of here. Are you good to go home?" she asked.

"Yeah, sure," Camila replied. "Wait, what about your dad's book?"

"I… haven't finished with it yet. I'm going to give it to the police. I just need to see why Marigold would do this—why she would just take my dad from me."

"Hey, it's your choice. It's just… the longer you hold on to it, the more suspicious it will be," Camila said. "Anyway, I'm tired and need to just knock out. Are you sure you'll be okay alone? Why don't you stay here with your mother? That way, you can take care of each other. This is a hard time for you both."

"You're right. I was so in my own head and feelings, I didn't even think," Solei replied. "I'm going to check in on her, then take you home. I think I'll stay here to take care of her."

Solei

Solei wanted to object immediately when Camila made the suggestion, but then she thought about how her mother had acted, how she had been acting for several days now.

Solei's first reaction was typically to assume the worst in Luz, and now her stomach hurt with the thought that she hadn't even considered what this all meant for her mother. Her parents had been together for thirty-plus years. Luz waited on her dad hand and foot from the beginning, dealt with an affair, a child from that affair, and still remained with him. Now, he's gone.

Luz had a whole life ahead of her; she had a chain of successful businesses, she had love. The problem was that Solei didn't know if her mother knew that. Luz needed her, so her mother would be her priority.

As Solei ascended the steps, she paused to look at their family portraits. They were so happy in the photos, but now everything felt broken—empty. She couldn't go into her mother's room with a defeated mentality. Her mother emphasized strength. So she paused momentarily, gathered herself, and knocked on the door.

"Mama, it's Solei. I'd like to come in."

"*Pasa.*"

Solei pushed into the dimly lit room. The sight of her mother almost brought her to tears. Luz's face was smeared with makeup and her hair was disheveled. Solei didn't know where to start. Her prideful mother would not tolerate sympathy, but it was important that she be taken care of.

"Mama, I'm going to stay for a few days. Help take care of the house—and really—I need your company."

Luz looked up at her, and for the first time, Solei saw her mother. She saw the vulnerability that her mother was capable of, and she felt instantly closer to her. Solei hesitated for one second, then dropped onto the bed, engulfed in her mother's arms. For the first time, they wept together for all they had lost.

Chapter 17

Solei

Solei awoke to the sun peeking through her mother's curtains, and the warmth of her mother resting next to her. She imagined that her mother would dread the empty bed soon to come, but for now, she would fill the void of her mother's forthcoming loneliness.

Typically, she loved waking to the warmth of the sun, but today was not a day she wanted to face. She didn't want to face her father's death and the pending case, and more importantly… she didn't want the love and vulnerability of the night with her mom to end.

For once, Luz wasn't pretending—pretending to be strong, pretending to know what to do next. Her mother stirred and smiled. She would put her mother first as no one else ever seemed to.

Her mother leaned in to kiss her forehead.

"Buenos días, Mama," Solei said, smiling.

They lay there in the aftermath of a new reality—this one moment of solidarity.

"Want some breakfast, Mama? I can make whatever you want," Solei asked.

Luz smiled again. "That sounds nice, *mi hija*. I'll have whatever… and coffee."

Solei's face turned up at her mother's request. Luz had given up coffee in favor of Alberto's preference for tea, which they had for breakfast, lunch, and dinner.

Her mother winced, then said barely above a whisper, "I'm sorry."

Solei rummaged around the kitchen for breakfast items. The kitchen was in utter disorder. One of Luz's favored teacup sets was missing; it wasn't in the dishwasher or the cabinet. Luz doted over that family set which had been passed down for years. It perpetually sat next to the tea kettle. Now, it was nowhere to be found. Even the items in the cabinet were out of their usual places.

Luz was a stickler; everything had a place and everything should be in it. Every canned food item—although not many—was out of sorts, along with all spices and the decanter jar. The different kinds of pasta were scattered throughout the pantry, favored spices were not in the correct Lazy Susan, even the eggs hadn't been pilfered from their carton as usual and placed in the glass egg holder that her mother kept in the refrigerator.

Solei tamped down the lumps that rose in her throat. It was her mother who designated these places. It was the twenty-something years of her mother never deviating that brought Solei's nails to scrape at her palm. When one of her nails pulled at a fresh scab, she abruptly stopped. Closing her eyes, she took a few deep breaths and cleared her mind as best she could. *Not everything deserves a reaction. Not everything deserves my energy*, she thought, reminding herself of Camila's words.

Solei opened her eyes and looked down at the items she had collected thus far. "Coffee," she whispered and set about to search for some. First, she looked where the tea was typically kept, finding nothing but assorted teas and honeys.

Then, she checked the pantry, eyeballing the wide, long shelves. She found two jars of Bustelo. *Jackpot.* She began to pull at each lid, not wanting to open one if the other was already used. The first revealed an intact foil lid. When Solei pulled back the second lid, she saw large wads of crisp one-hundred-dollar bills.

Hmm. Her parents had a joint account or two. Her father made the money; her mother managed it. *Money in a can—like a regular person?* As she placed the lid back on the shelf, her mother's sudden appearance startled her.

"What the hell is that?" Luz said before the two erupted in laughter.

"Mama, hi—I haven't even started breakfast yet. And I was going to ask you the same," Solei said.

"I'm a proper lady. My runaway money is in a secret bank account," Luz said.

They looked at each other and burst into more uninhibited and raucous laughter filling the corners of their home. When the two were able to catch their breath, tears began to spill from their eyes—tears of joy and of sorrow for what they had lost to gain this moment.

"*Te amo*," Luz finally said.

"I love you, too, Mama."

As Solei reached for the coffee, Luz said, "It must have been your father's. Take it. You were the true love of his life, and I know he'd want you to have it."

And there it was—two jabs from Luz, except for once neither was toward Solei, and one jab seemed aimed at herself.

Chapter 18

Camila

Camila awoke in the darkness of her childhood bedroom, the blackout curtains doing their job. There was a dull throb in her temples, and her stomach was wringing from the lack of calories in her body. She needed to eat, but instead rolled over to grab the water and pain meds she received at the hospital. She wanted the numbness and high that she got from pain meds on an empty stomach. It had been a long week, and it was only downhill from there.

The police visit to the Quispes' house had put a wrench in things. She was supposed to be waking up—several hours from now—to Solei's amazing cooking, and their plan for more prying and digging into Berto's shenanigans. Now… there was the threat of Anna Sanchez. Any moment, the salsa music would start, and her mother would be in here to throw open the blinds and demand that she did something useful with herself. Never mind her concussion or that she felt like absolute shit, if Camila wasn't going to work, she had to at least be productive.

Camila wasn't sure why she opted to come here instead of her own place. Then she realized her senses got the better of her last night. She'd felt like shit, and the nurse's warnings echoed in her mind. Scared to go home and utterly exhausted, she instinctively put her parents' address into her **GPS**. *At least there would be breakfast*, she thought as Spanish music filtered in under the door from the hallway. Surprisingly, the music was low so Camila thanked God for small wins.

She flipped onto her back. There were things to be done. Then, a memory pinged in her mind. The agenda pages. She rolled over with a galumph, reached over the side of her bed, and felt around in her bag. She wasn't quite ready to turn the light on, and for several minutes she struggled to locate the small, carefully folded pages. Her fingers finally grazed the sharp corner of the lump.

Camila turned onto her belly, angled her phone's flashlight against her chest and at the pages, then carefully unfolded them. She skimmed through the pages, satisfied she had them all. Camila questioned herself; she had no remorse for ripping them out, or for betraying her best friend's confidence. Solei was no doubt already feeling betrayed by the most important people in her life and needed to have at least one person to trust. It had to be Camila.

After years of friendship, quietly examining and interacting with Solei, Camila knew she was on the brink. Solei was one more "upset" from having a nervous breakdown. And now that her father's body was found and identified, Camila knew even more so what would happen if Solei broke down now. The police wouldn't even bother looking for the truth; they'd assume it was her.

Camila got back to the task at hand. Although she had already ripped the pages out, she was hard-pressed to destroy them. She wanted nothing more than to rip them into a million pieces and throw them into a fire, but needed to keep tabs on information that might come into play. *Why do I need to read these over and over?*

The first page had angry red lines that underlined the words **CAMILA SAW US!!** *Was he scared? Guilty?* The idea that Alberto could feel guilt was new to her.

Solei didn't see it—she couldn't—the way Alberto hurt Luz, but Camila could. Maybe it was her schooling, her training, that equipped her with the tools to spot psychological abuse. The truth was Camila saw it go both ways with Solei's family. They both hurt each other in small and big ways, but to Camila, Alberto was the worst offender. She also understood her own biases. The one true thing she knew about her biological father was that he wasn't there for her. So, maybe Alberto wasn't the worst of the two, but at least Luz kept her shortcomings private and at home.

Three times she saw Alberto in public with another woman. Each time, she grew more and more convinced that he was just a terrible person.

Camila had wanted to tell Solei each time she saw Alberto with Marigold but never knew how. Each instance made the previous one seem like a betrayal on Camila's part. With each new instance, she didn't know how to justify not telling Solei about the last. Then, once Solei had the agenda, Camila knew immediately what she had to do. Sure, Solei could have seen the entries already, but Camila highly doubted it. Her parents were the only people Solei concealed her emotions from. With everything that had happened yesterday, it was too late to confess now.

Something lurked in the recesses of Camila's mind. She tried to stamp it down along with the anxiety—part denial and part fear. She didn't want to even think about it, let alone say it out loud. The police were investigating everyone involved, and Camila was questioning her own motives once again. She wanted to trust her version of events. As she replayed that day in her mind, her bedroom door opened.

"*Mi hija*, you okay?" her mother asked. Anna wore her white and blue floral *bata*, curlers in her dark brown tresses, and a spatula in hand. Something good was cooking. Camila slowly tucked the pages under her pillow and turned to face her mother.

"*Ta bien*, mama. I'm pretty hungry, though," Camila said with a broad smile. She was grateful to have her tumultuous thoughts interrupted, and her mother's food made everything better. She didn't care what her mother had cooked at this point. Anna smiled, then used pursed lips to point in the direction of the kitchen. Camila frowned, remembering she had to break the news to her parents.

Alberto and her father weren't the best of friends, but they hung out from time to time. Camila wasn't sure how to even broach the subject. She knew the dramatics that would ensue once she explained that someone involved in her accident was the culprit.

Uncharacteristically, Camila ate in silence at the table with her family. She kept her eyes turned downward and focused on the bright red tablecloth. With each passing minute, she noticed her mother and father sharing glances. They had no doubt noticed her silence, but for some reason were reluctant to break it themselves. By now, Anna would have asked her daughter what was wrong several times. Camila wondered if they were giving her space because she was injured, or if there was something else going on. Finally, Camila broke the silence.

"There's been news." She paused, collecting the right words in her head.

"Is it your health? Are you okay?" Anna already sounded panicked.

"Mama, please. Just let me get it out. Except for a massive headache, I am fine. During the crash cleanup, police found a body," Camila said, wincing. Her mother's small yelp gave her pause before she continued, "In the trunk of a car belonging to someone named Marigold was Mr. Quispe's body. I'm sorry. There's more. The driver, Marigold, is supposedly the love child of Alberto from an affair he had years ago." Camila wasn't sure she should have added the last bit, but she didn't want them to find out in an impersonal way.

Her mother gasped as she and Manny said "Dios mío," in unison. Then, she broke into a full sob. Manny shook his head, his eyes welling up.

He stood up and wrapped his arms around his wife. Camila placed her hands around her mother's, giving them a light squeeze. "Let me take you to bed, mi amor," Manny finally said. Anna looked up at her husband and he instinctively wiped the tears from her cheeks. "Ta bien, ta bien," he

                    Negrón

murmured. As he helped his wife up, he gave Camila a look she understood to mean—stay put.

Camila slumped down in her chair, not sure how to feel about it all, and a bit confused as to what her father might want to speak with her about. She couldn't even try to prep herself to get her story straight—whatever "straight" was. So much had happened in the last few days that she hadn't planned for. Yes, she had a hand in some of the week's events. She just kept thinking of her last words to Marigold, and how that might look to the police. A part of her knew Marigold must be incapacitated in some way, based on the questions the detectives had asked. *What could she tell them about me?* Camila thought.

"I can see your brain turning," Manny said as he reentered the room. "Let's talk, because I already know what you're thinking. I'm very sorry for his family, but it's not your fault, Camila. There's nothing you could have done. You were one among many folks in that car crash."

"You weren't there, papa. When the police came and told Luz and Solei, I mean. You didn't see their devastation. I'm sad for their family, but I'm pissed for my friend. She never even got to confront him for the lies. He's dodged Solei for weeks. You know how she found out about the affair and the other child?" Camila paused, wondering if she was going too far. She shared a lot with her father, but somehow she felt telling would put him in the thick of things. A part of her also felt like the less her father knew, the safer he might be.

Camila couldn't meet Manny's eyes. She saw the look he gave her, so full of love, but she could tell he understood—she had said more than she wanted to. He gave her an almost imperceptible nod; she knew she could tell him as much or as little as she needed to in this moment. She pleaded with her eyes, trying to tell him without words, *When I'm ready I'll tell you everything.*

Chapter 19

Solei

As Solei and Luz sat to eat a late breakfast, the weight of Alberto's absence settled in his empty chair. Solei's mother no longer had to serve her father, or make his tea just right, or wait for his silent nod of satisfaction before sitting down to eat her own food. Solei was sure that Luz's silence wasn't a refusal to talk. She met her mother's eyes across the table, and they exchanged weak smiles. The two ate in silence, the camaraderie of the morning slowly evaporating.

Luz finally spoke. "I'm going to grab a shower, *mi hija.* Then, we can start making calls and arrangements." She stood up from the table with a sigh, her dark tresses swishing around her. "There's much to be done while we wait for them to return your beloved father to us." At that, Luz scraped her plate into the garbage, rinsed it, then placed it in the dishwasher.

Solei pushed the remnants of the brunch around her plate. Her mother's callousness had returned like the sting of a cold, wet wind. It was as if the moments, the shared love, the perceived progress between them had never happened.

When Solei heard the shower running, she rose quickly and scurried to the home office. She ripped open drawers, rummaging through every folder, periodically listening for her mother. Solei was determined to find the letter.

The letter was stuffed into an unlabeled folder under a pile of obscure papers thrown into a drawer. "Here you are." A week ago, she would have worried that the messy drawer was so unlike her mother, but now she questioned everything she thought she knew about Luz Ramirez-Quispe. *Why hide it? Why lie? Had you read the letter? You knew Dad hadn't told Marigold who he really was.* Her mind filled with unanswered questions, and she wanted to shake the truth out of her mother.

***

Solei sat in her car staring daggers at the front of her parents' home. She needed Camila.

She looked up once more to make sure her mother hadn't come out to look for her. Solei intended to re-read the letter for clues—clues of what she didn't know. The photograph of Marigold had not been with the letter, but the envelope had. What she really hoped to find was the envelope's address, but there was no proof it had ever seen the inside of a post office. The envelope contained no return address or postage; it didn't even have her parents' address on it. Just Alberto Quispe written on the front.

"Dammit!" Solei yelled, punching the steering wheel. In her rage, she accidentally triggered Bluetooth, so she instructed it to call Camila. She stuffed the letter back in the envelope, then into the sandwich bag and her glove compartment.

"Hey," Camila answered.

"Oh, good, you're not at work. Wait… why aren't you at work?"

"I'm okay… at my parents'. Just need a little more time dealing with my own things before I go back to healing the world," Camila said.

"Okay, sooo… where to start? I felt like my mother and I were really connecting, but… maybe we're just broken. We sat there eating the first meal of the rest of our lives without my dad and there was something in my mother's eyes. She looked—I don't know—at peace rather than distraught. My father, her husband, was murdered. And I couldn't stop thinking about her lying to the police."

"Wait, what? What did she lie about?" Camila asked.

"The letter. Remember? I found it on their desk when I went to help her organize the office. There's no way she didn't see it. Now that I think of it, there was a damn letter opener stabbed into the desk. I highly doubt that was my dad." Even as Solei said those last words, she understood that she knew less than she ever thought about either of her parents. She never thought her father would cheat, or ignore her, or have the audacity to meet a love child behind his *real* family's back.

"Earth to Solei. Are you okay? Did you hear what I said?" Camila asked.

"*Perdón.* I didn't hear anything you said. My mind is reeling. Then, after breakfast, she just said, 'I'm gonna take a shower, then we'll make arrangements.' Like, my father is dead! She hasn't asked once how I'm feeling. God! I just fu—I just can't," Solei yelled into the Bluetooth. Her head was spinning; she had to calm down. She was hyperventilating, and her lips were beginning to numb.

Solei cracked the window, took several deep breaths, and said, "I'm sorry. I just… What were you saying?"

"Nothing, it's not important. I'm so sorry for your loss, *amiga*. Please take it easy. The funeral arrangements will probably only exacerbate the way you're feeling right now, so take some time to self-soothe."

After several more minutes, Camila made a few excuses and clicked off the line.

Solei contemplated what to do next. The last thing she wanted to do was callously go over funeral arrangements for her murdered father, but the last time she whisked off, all hell broke loose. This time, she would carry out her father's last wishes.

Chapter 20

Detective Rose

The detectives sat in silence. Rose thought this case would be cleaner. The motive for their prime suspect was just handed to them… along with two more suspects to look into. Maybe three.

"Are you hungry? A few slices from Pronto's sounds like the jam right now," Rose said, trying to clear his mind. He needed to pull all the pieces back into the framework of this new information—there was a mistress, a wife who paid her to disappear, and three jaded women. They did their best brainstorming over food and in a casual setting as opposed to the office.

"I could eat," Hamilton replied.

"You realize we now have at least three more suspects, right?" Rose asked.

"Honestly, a twice-scorned wife sounds like a hell of a lot better motive than a long-lost daughter."

"What about the biological daughter? Not only did she find out her dad cheated, but then he dodges her for the new daughter… her hero's character is tarnished."

"Okay, Dr. Rose," Hamilton said, laughing too loudly. "Honestly, there's something about the best friend. I just don't trust her."

"This is why I need pizza." Hamilton retorted.

After ordering a few slices, both detectives sat down in the far corner of the pizzeria, hopefully out of earshot of the only other patron. The dining area of the pizzeria was small with only two tables flanking either side of the door, and three booths on the wall opposite the counter. The walls were lined with photographs of different bridges and buildings in New York.

"So, Alberto Quispe, owner of several successful custom perfume shops, married to Luz and having one child, Solei. Then, man meets another woman, has an affair, but wants to stay with wife and daughter. Fast forward a few months, and the mistress comes to their home to tell him she's pregnant but is sent away by the wife, probably with money. Am I missing anything so far?" Rose paused, flipping back and forth through his notes.

"Nope," Hamilton replied. "Then, fast forward several years, Marigold's mother is what… sick, remorseful, and decides Alberto should know about his long-lost daughter. You know, to give them a chance to get to know each other. Only, she tells Alberto via letter? How could she guarantee he'd get it? That Luz wouldn't take the letter and burn it up?"

"Somehow, he gets it, but not at his house, per the wife, and decides to meet his daughter. Hides it from his wife. Boy, this guy was an effing gem. Meets with his long-lost daughter, Marigold, but doesn't tell her who he really is for what? Weeks… months? That's kind of creepy. What did Marigold think they were doing all of this time?" Rose asked. It seemed like a golden piece of information as soon as it came out of Luz's mouth, though Rose couldn't understand why.

The slices came over, and they ate in silence.

"You know what we need," Rose said between chews. "Well, besides Marigold waking the hell up… we need to get inside Alberto's head."

Hamilton laughed. "There are too many missing pieces now. Some of it—like Hunter's side of it all—we may get, but then there's the letter. The letter connected Alberto to his alleged killer and is possibly a link to other players," Hamilton started to say.

"Like Hunter's mother. Who we also don't really have the identity of?" Rose interjected.

"Yes, like Hunter's mother. It would be helpful to know when he received this letter, and where it originated. We wanted a motive, now we have too many. What would Marigold have to gain… especially if she didn't know that Quispe was her father?" Hamilton asked.

"Yes, but that's assuming she didn't know. Doesn't seem like Quispe was that open with his wife. Alberto is wealthy, right? The man owns several stores across the country. Now that the death notification has been made, there will undoubtedly be a will, right? We can't know for sure if he told Luz about any will changes, but either way, the will thickens the plot. I know plenty of women who would snap if their husband changed the will without so much as a discussion."

Chapter 21

Camila

As the treads of her shoes ripped into the dirt path, Camila could feel the heat rising from her thigh muscles, through her torso and throat, until she felt the burn in her face. She didn't get runner's high like others, but then again, she didn't always run for peace. This time, anger pushed her to rise, dress, and hit the pavement. She jogged on the concrete, knowing her body yearned for the slip and grab of a dirt path. Her mind raced as she approached the state park, navigating the chaos of fallen trees and the divots of the unpaved path.

Solei's call had triggered Camila's painful childhood memories. Flashes of two-person family dinners that were underpinned with sorrow. Camila remembered the empty, long stares of her biological mother as she mentally traipsed through time with her long, lost beloved—the lows she would reach before she snapped back into the present and back into his absence.

Camila ran faster.

She turned off the main trail—the white birches growing closer together and the path becoming more treacherous. With each burst of sunlight, she recalled her mother's tantrum-like outbursts. Everything, all of their lack, could be attributed to *his* absence. Camila tried to control her breathing, but each jump was followed by a sharp flash of memory. The one she loved and hated most—her eighth birthday—was yet to play. The last childhood birthday she'd spend with her mother, who would no longer find her way back from depression. It was the last birthday before her mother decided Camila was better off being raised by someone else.

Camila shook off the memory, not wanting the emotional shitstorm that rained down after. As the wind picked up, she ripped the tie from her ponytail and let her hair whip out behind her. She pumped her arms and legs harder. *Men only hurt us if we let them,* she decided. She'd always been enraged at the man who used, then threw away, her mother. She was angry at her mother for letting herself be hurt, and worse, choosing that anger as an occupant—no, a dependent—more important than her own daughter. Camila was also angry at Alberto for hurting everyone around her. And Camila decided she was mad *for* Solei… and at Luz.

Chapter 22

Rose

The Homicide Department was crammed with four computer-clad desks along the walls on either side of the room, a small room that housed the captain's office at the head, and a large dry-erase board stretched down the middle. The board was littered with scribblings of statistics and case notes. Rose and Hamilton's metal desks sat parallel at opposite walls.

Rose slammed the phone onto the receiver and was already swiping his traveler's notebook off the desk when Hamilton looked up. His demeanor gave way to something big. He swiveled in his chair to face his partner and smiled. "She's awake."

The duo had eagerly waited for Marigold Hunter to rise because nothing in this case was making sense. How Marigold came to meet Alberto, the nature of their relationship, and why she would purposely cause an accident with her murder victim in the trunk.

Rose was convinced Marigold was the culprit, and wanted to shut the case down, but Hamilton pushed back. This was one of the reasons their partnership worked—friendly, confrontational interplay. Hamilton's ability to think far out of the box, along with her take-no-shit-but-be-kind demeanor, made her a better detective. Everyone at the precinct called Rose the "Bull," wincing away from any confrontation with him, but Hamilton called him out every time.

"Okay, Jack, we need to tread lightly here. To be strategic. We cannot do things the good ol' Bully way. This woman is either very smart, or very insane, but either way—she is fragile. If she is the killer, we don't want to give her any outs," Hamilton said.

"I'd go with the latter, but unfortunately, I agree about our approach here. My gut says it was her simply because the body was in her trunk, but there is so much more to consider now." Rose admitted.

"How about we start with simply asking her about the nature of their relationship? Find out who *she* thinks Alberto is… before telling her we found his body in her trunk."

"Sounds like a plan," Rose agreed.

***

Outside of Marigold's hospital room, Rose and Hamilton flashed their badges for the police officer outside the door. Hamilton lightly rapped on the door, then pushed it open. "Ms. Hunter? We're Detective Hamilton and Detective Rose. We're just here to ask a few questions."

The knock was a formality, a courtesy in case the woman was indecent. As they pushed further into the room, Marigold scooted up in the bed. Her auburn hair was disheveled, there was a pallor to her skin, and she had bags under her eyes.

"Apologies for my appearance, but…" Marigold trailed off, lifting her handcuffed arm. "Maybe you can tell me why I'm cuffed. Wasn't I in a car wreck?" Her voice grew callous and smug.

"We'll get to that, Ms. Hunter," Rose replied.

"We have a few questions, if you don't mind," Hamilton said, shooting Rose a warning look. "Ms. Hunter, can you please tell me about your relationship with one Alberto Quispe?"

Marigold visibly quivered at the mention of the name. She drew the blanket to her chest, despite the room being warm. The young woman slowly closed her eyes, took an audible breath, then set her gaze on Hamilton. "There's no way to dress it up. He's my lover… Well, it's more of a romantic friendship… until he left his wife. We didn't sleep together… or even kiss, really. It's more of a friendship with… romantic underpinnings. He's leaving his wife, though," Marigold stuttered. "I know I sound like one of those girls, but Alberto is different."

Rose's mouth dropped open at this revelation. Hamilton shook her head.

Marigold's raspy voice broke the silence. "Is… everything okay?" she asked.

"I'm afraid not," Rose tutted. "Ms. Hunter, you're referring to Mr. Quispe in the present tense, but… we're here because the car crash revealed his body in your car's trunk."

Marigold quietly gasped, and her mouth moved, but no words came out. Her shoulders slumped as if she were caught. Rose wanted to tell her that they could prove that her duvet covered his body, that his DNA on her hallway floor proved his body was in her house, but even he knew better than to interrupt a suspect on the verge of confessing. There was fear, confusion, and misery in her eyes.

"Ms. Hunter… can I call you Marigold? Did you hear us?" Hamilton gently coaxed. "Can you tell us how you met Mr. Quispe? How you came to be lovers?"

Marigold vomited her words. "I wouldn't call us lovers, per se. We never slept together. Never kissed. We met one day while I was on a shift at a small café in Luzerne, where I work part-time. He sat at one of my tables and struck up a conversation. He was so sweet—gentlemanly. He didn't hit on me, but you know… mildly flirted. I chalked it up to him being a bit older… maybe not knowing *how to* flirt. Before I knew it, we were having lunches and early dinners. I would never hurt him; I loved him."

Hamilton and Rose exchanged a glance.

"He told me about his wife, but it was more like… he talked about her more like a past memory, like a woman he no longer really understood. I… I didn't kill him. I didn't have a reason to. The last time I saw him was Friday, I swear," Marigold pleaded, stifling tears. "We were supposed to meet at the café. He said there was something he had to tell me. I… I thought he was finally leaving his wife. That we would be… it doesn't matter. He never even came in. I watched him take off. But that's not a motive… I understood, you know."

Rose raised an eyebrow.

Hamilton continued her line of questioning. "Understood? It didn't upset you, perhaps, that he didn't come in? That he may have gotten… cold feet."

"He left because his daughter was there," Marigold said, lowering her eyes.

Rose unintentionally popped his gum. The case was like a batting cage on fast pitch. Curveball after fastball.

"I didn't know. I've never met her, but a few minutes before I saw him leave, a young woman—around my age, I think—approached me. She said something like, 'he's not who you think he is.' Poor girl probably saw me as some kind of homewrecker. But that's not what it was. I swear." Marigold sighed. "Anyway, yes, I was upset… I was pissed, okay, that he blew me off, but maybe his daughter being there spooked him, okay. Of course, he had to leave. Yes, she's an adult, but still. I would be devastated if my parents divorced."

This was the cue to insert the truth. It was now or never. Hamilton gave Rose a soft nod.

Rose softened his face, and said with an empathetic smile, "Ms. Hunter… Marigold. Alberto Quispe thought he was your biological father."

Marigold blurted, "I'm sorry. What? No. What?" Her forehead dampened. "My father is Desmond Hunter. Why do you think that? No.... Alberto was my…" Marigold couldn't bring herself to finish the sentence. Her mouth moved, but no words came out, and she began to gag. Her monitors began to beep wildly, making Rose jump as Hamilton's face registered concern.

Rose blurted, "We're going to run a DNA test for our investigation. Is that okay with you?"

Just as the nurse burst into the room, Marigold yelled, "Yes! Take my DNA. He was not my—"

The nurse intercepted. "It may be best to end the interview here until I have time to confer with the doctor," she said, feeding a sedative into Marigold intravenously.

Marigold's body softened as the drugs took their effect.

The detectives stepped out of the room, waiting for the nurse. When the nurse emerged, Rose gave her a stern look. "We need a DNA sample ASAP. Either your patient is dangerous, or she's in way over her head."

Chapter 23

Solei

Solei took a final deep breath, gathering her nerve, then stuffed the envelope and letter back into her glove compartment. Her mother beckoned. Solei plastered on a weak smile, hugged Luz, and followed her inside.

"Okay, so I made a list of *familia* we need to call, and in what order. Here is yours—it's shorter. When you're done," Luz said, pointing to the bottom half of the page, "I need you to call the funeral home and make an appointment. I've already called Father Vicente. How many days can you take off of work?"

"My boss said I can take the week off, but to let her know if I needed more time," Solei said matter-of-factly. She felt both annoyed and appreciative of her mother's systematic nature. There were so many feelings boiling over in every limb that she needed the callousness.

Solei moved from the foyer to the *sala*; the room looked different. A serape was draped over the couch, and matching patterned coasters sat on the coffee table. The wall above the couch—which was sparsely adorned—was now littered with traditional Peruvian motifs. Her mother's least favorite tea set—a gift from Solei's paternal grandmother—was out on the table with all the appropriate accompaniments. The house had suddenly adopted her father's sense of ethnic pride.

And the show begins, Solei thought. She cringed and sighed, but prepared herself a cup of tea and found a cozy spot to make her calls. Her mother had graciously supplied a notepad and pencils. Solei followed closely as Luz made her way down the hall to the office.

***

Solei eyed Luz, who sat perfectly poised and upright at Alberto's desk. Her teacup was nestled in its saucer, notebook neatly folded under itself, and pencils all in a row. She took a small sip of her tea, shook out her hair, and picked up her phone. She looked like a businesswoman about to enter an important meeting rather than a grieving wife. Solei understood that everyone grieves differently, but this was a lot… even for her mother.

Luz made the first call, and though she spoke at a lower volume than Solei could make out, her tone was clear and monotonous as she broke the news to someone in what seemed like a rehearsed string of words.

Alternatively, Solei prepared to make her first phone call and scanned the names on her list. With the exception of her paternal grandparents, everyone was on her father's side of the family. *Damn it, Ma.* All Solei could think was, of course, she doesn't want to speak with them. Her father's side was admittedly more emotional than her mother's, and her mother just couldn't be bothered to deal with any tears or sobbing.

Solei knew the Ramirezes' true feelings about her late father—they didn't believe he was good enough for her mother. A part of her hated to admit that they were at least partially correct in their assumptions, although for the wrong reasons.

Solei made the funeral home appointment first. She wanted to be coherent when making that call, and inevitably having to explain that they did not have the body yet. How do you explain that your father was murdered, and they're still investigating, so they're holding on to him for the foreseeable future?" *And oh yeah, we're the most likely suspects, too.*

Luz erupted in a loud, raucous burst of laughter that almost made Solei vomit. She had had enough.

Solei made her calls, giving each person a respectable amount of time to grieve over the phone, then politely excused herself from the conversation with a final condolence and the need to call *los otros queridos familiares.* When she was done with her last call, she stormed over to Luz's desk.

Luz looked up, giving Solei a stern look. Solei was surprised to see tears in her mother's eyes as she covered the mouthpiece of the phone and mouthed, *tú eres loca.* Solei laid the notebook on the desk and walked out.

She was pushing it. Her mother was not above giving her a *cocotaso,* but she also knew Luz would not dare interrupt whatever family member was on the other end. Solei was too scared and angry to look back at her mother. She walked swiftly through the sala and foyer, collecting her things before heading to her car.

As Solei drove away, she kept looking back in the rearview mirror, somewhat expecting her mother to be standing out there, waving her fists in the air. That was her mother's universal "you're gonna get it" move, but Solei found only the wisp of the house through her teary eyes.

She needed to talk to her best friend.

Chapter 24

Camila

Camila's phone buzzed before she had a chance to put it on "Do Not Disturb." She had a client arriving in about an hour, but needed to get a set of misplaced records back to their home. Paralyzed by the fear of being caught replacing them, she let the phone buzz. Finally, it stopped going off for a few seconds, then chimed the arrival of a voicemail. Camila looked down and saw Solei's name flash on the screen. She should at least listen to the message. The last part of her best friend's words traveled through the phone speaker, causing Camila's grip to tighten. "You have to help me meet Marigold."

Her mouth grew dry; this was more fodder for the slaughter. It was only a matter of time before her patient arrived, and she needed a moment to gather her composure.

Camila stood up and shook herself, letting her arms flail before falling to meet her toes. She repeated this motion, all the while taking several deep breaths. The image of wind whipping her hair up as she sped faster through an imaginary wood played over and over in her mind.

Ignoring Solei's call would have one of two effects. Solei would either devolve emotionally or she'd get angry. Camila prayed for the latter. Her friend should be angry, though not with her. *Or maybe I'm the perfect person to be mad at.*

Solei's admissions as of late still trudged through Camila's mind. She couldn't believe that Luz would lie to the police so openly. Admittedly, she could not put it past the woman either. She had turned away a pregnant woman, then kept the child from Alberto and Solei for years.

There was also the way Luz reacted to the news of his death. She didn't ask any questions—not really. Nor did she cry or demand to see his body. Solei probably had more to tell, and that's why she called, but now was not the time.

As Camila took a long sip of her coffee, there was a knock at the door. Her client wasn't due for another several minutes, and she silently prayed it wasn't Solei doing a pop-in. Before she could have a chance to tell the person to come in, her boss stepped through the door. His bearded, cherub face and rolled-up dress shirt sleeves belied his demeanor. Camila hesitated as he stepped in with a stern look. She braced herself for the berating or possible termination of her time there, but his wide grin cracked.

"I'm sorry… you should have seen your face. It was priceless. What're you doing, playing one of those computer games or something?" he asked mockingly. He shoved his chubby hands into the pockets of his khakis, rocking back and forth on his suffering loafers.

"No sir, just a rough few days. I found out my best friend's father… really—like a father to me—has passed. And in the most tragic of ways."

"Oh, dear. Why don't you take the rest of the day off? Your last client actually canceled for the day anyway."

"I'd like that," Camila said, relieved.

Camila made a mental checklist as her boss left the room. She needed time to get her bearings, to try to figure out how to confess it all to Solei. How could she tell her best friend that she saw her deceased father the day before his murder? That she saw Marigold and confronted her?

As Camila walked out toward the door, she almost forgot about the traveling file she had to put back. It was too early for that today; she had hoped to work late and sneak it back then, but that wasn't possible now. It was the most important move she had to make… before anyone noticed. She decided to duck out for a few hours, then come back later that night.

She didn't bother turning her phone back on. She needed time to think, undisturbed and unclouded by other people's problems.

Chapter 25

Detective Rose

Rose swished left to right in his chair, his eyebrows knitted together. He had gone into the interview ready to press Marigold hard, but now he was questioning his conviction. Her version of their relationship added yet another turbid layer. *Why did she think she and the victim were lovers?*

Rose had to get out of his head. He tore off the notepad paper he'd been scribbling on, crumpled it, then tossed it at his partner, who looked deep in thought as well. When she looked up, he asked, "So, where the hell do we start today?"

"Are you also confused as to how Quispe thought he was getting to know his long-lost daughter, while his long-lost daughter thought they were having an affair?" Hamilton asked, raising her eyebrows.

"Um, yeah. And maybe that's where we start. Hunter said they were meeting at her job that day, and something tells me that wasn't the first time. Why don't we talk to her co-workers to see if anyone can tell us about those meetings?" Rose suggested.

"Perfect. We can also corroborate her story. Did she meet up with him on Friday or not? Did anyone see her talking to a woman matching Solei's description…" Hamilton trailed off.

"So, I was thinking we start with verifying the basics—does Hunter actually work there? Was she working Friday night or Saturday morning? Was she there outside of work hours or any other time with a man?" Rose smiled. Hamilton laid out the safe questions, but he would push the limits with the hard and messy ones. His partner could get feisty, but she liked to be cool-headed.

"I think that's perfect," Hamilton said with a chuckle. "Now what do you really want to ask? The person we're talking to will dictate who gets to ask the juicy questions."

"Well, then we'll ask if they saw her Friday with a man. Did she leave with that man? How many times has anyone seen her with him? Do we have a photograph of Quispe? We could have pulled one from—" Rose was cut off by Hamilton pulling out a printout of Alberto from one of his social media accounts. The two exchanged a smile.

"We should also talk to the officer. What was his name again? Miles—Miles Simmons? He might have some insight," Hamilton said.

"We'll talk to him when we get back," Rose replied as his partner sped down the Cross Valley.

***

The smell of chamomile, lavender, and scones made Rose's stomach growl as they walked into the café. Each table was adorned with a vinyl tablecloth and a vase of fall florals.

Save for a few scattered patrons, the place was rather empty.

As they approached the counter, a bubbly brunette in an apron turned with a smile. "Welcome to *Tea, Read, Love*. How can I help you?"

Hamilton took a cursory glance around, ensuring no one was waiting behind them, then asked, "We need to speak with the manager."

"Preferably the one who was on duty last Friday," Rose added.

"Devin is the manager—the only manager. He's basically here every day," she said, her grin stretching across her face. "If you'd like to have a seat at that far table," she said, pointing, "I can bring you a coffee and scone while you wait—on the house, of course."

Before Hamilton could decline, Rose shot her a look that almost made her laugh. The detectives walked over and sat at the table she had pointed to. It was tucked in an alcove that offered privacy from nosy ears, yet remained open enough for the manager to feel comfortable joining them.

The detectives sat on the same side of the long table. Rose kept looking towards the counter. He needed a cup of good coffee. A moment later, a young man brought over their refreshments.

"Do you know Marigold?" Hamilton asked.

"Do I know her?" the waiter said, his eyes gleaming and a wide grin spreading across his face. "She hasn't been in… not since, you know," the waiter trailed off, looking around. "We're all wondering if it has to do with that juicy professor-type she's been bringing in here. I mean, I don't know if he's a professor. He just has that look to him, ya know. I've seen the news, ya know. So tragic. And craaaaazy," he said. "I can't believe there was a…" The waiter stopped when he saw the approaching manager, a tall, thin Black man with a polo tucked into khakis.

"I'm famished. I'll order more after we talk to your manager," Hamilton said, winking at the waiter, who grinned and walked off.

"Hi, Devin," the manager announced with an inflection in his voice. "Paola said you wanted to speak with me. I'm assuming about Marigold." He looked like he was going to say something else but changed his mind.

"Hi, Devin, I'm Detective Benita Hamilton, and this is my partner, Jack Rose. We just have a few questions about Ms. Hunter. Have a seat."

Devin obliged, sitting down at the table.

"So, Ms. Hunter worked here?" Rose asked.

"She's worked here for about two and a half years. Really, she's been a model employee—never late, works hard, customers love her, never messes up an order, takes on extra shifts. I was extremely surprised to see that news report," Devin said, shaking his head.

"Did Marigold work on Friday—at any point—or Saturday morning?" Hamilton followed up.

"She was here on Friday, early afternoon, but she didn't have a shift. She did have a shift Saturday morning but called out. I'd have to double check, but I'm pretty sure that was only the second time she ever called out. The other was when her mother got sick."

Hamilton and Rose exchanged a look and took notes.

"And Friday. Was she here alone?" Rose asked.

"She was alone, but she seemed to be waiting for someone. I didn't see when she left, but throughout the time she was here, she kept checking her phone, and… looking out of the window," Devin's eyebrows furrowed. "I would speak with Paola and Jayce, the waiter. They were on that day and may have seen more than I did." Devin was already getting up as he waved Jayce over to the detectives. Hamilton turned to see Jayce enthusiastically approaching.

"Thank you, Devin. We'll be in touch if we have any more questions," Hamilton said, shaking his hand as he scurried off.

As Jayce returned to their table, Rose prompted, "So, you were saying… about a professor-type."

"Oh my goodness. Yeah, so he was a little older than I would go for. Ya know, right on the other side of older and old guy. Anyway, for the past few months maybe, he comes in, sits at Goldie's table; they chat up. I've seen them meet up for lunch and dinner as well—though they don't do much eating. She tries to pretend it's nothing, but why else would they spend so much time together? He ain't her dad."

Rose snorted, making his partner shoot him a dirty look.

Hamilton interjected. "So, Friday. Did you see Ms. Hunter?"

"Yeah. She was here. Looked like she was waiting. I didn't see when she left. We were pretty busy, and my tables are back here. Paola might've seen something. She was working the register," Jayce concluded, gesturing to their empty coffee cups.

"I think we're all done here. Thank you," Hamilton replied as Jayce smiled and moved to tend another table.

The detectives walked over to the register, slowing to give Paola time to finish with a customer. Paola was their last chance to find out if Marigold had met up with Alberto that day. When Paola was free, and it didn't look like anyone else would come to her register, Hamilton asked, "Hi, Paola. Us again. Did you see Ms. Hunter on Friday? Did she meet up here with anyone?"

"Um… yeah, she was here. She kept checking her phone, looking out the window. In the end, she ended up just leaving alone. There was some weird commotion outside, like umm, tires screeching. We were all—kind of—staring out of the window to see what was going on. Anyways, she ended up leaving way later. Oh, she did talk to a woman shortly before the commotion started."

At this, Rose perked up. This is what they technically came to find out. Knowing whether or not Marigold met up with Alberto was easy enough to find out… if they had a warrant. But they weren't there yet. He looked over at his partner to see if she was going to continue. Hamilton gave him a look.

"What did she look like—this other woman? Have you seen them here before?" Hamilton asked.

They would circle back to the outside commotion, but wanted to get a description of the person that followed Marigold while the girl had the fresh memory.

"So, she was probably my height—so like 5'7-ish. She had olive skin and dark hair. I don't remember serving her and didn't get a great look at her. She didn't seem to be the person Marigold was waiting for," Paola said, thoughtfully. "Oh, and yes, I think I've seen the other woman here before. It's hard to tell."

"How can you be sure Ms. Hunter wasn't waiting for her?" Rose asked.

"Marigold was still checking her phone when the other woman came in. The other woman sat down with her back to Marigold, and they didn't speak until Marigold got up and headed for the bathroom. Anyway, I'm typically at the register, so I see patrons only briefly... unless they sit at these front tables."

"And the commotion outside. Did you see what was going on exactly?" Hamilton asked.

Rose contemplated Paola's words, having an inkling that it was important in more ways than he could fathom. He secretly hoped his partner was absorbing things as he took notes, and had picked up what he couldn't quite figure out.

"It was just some guy peeling off in some fancy dark blue car," Paola said.

Rose flipped rapidly through his notepad, then suddenly clicked his tongue and tapped the book with his pen.

"You sure it was dark blue? Was it an SUV? You don't have any clue as to what kind of car?" Rose spit out the questions fast, treading the line between asking and leading.

"Yes, it was really dark, but definitely blue. I've seen a similar car parked out front before, though I definitely couldn't tell you if it's the same one or what kind. It was something high-end." Rose and Hamilton waited with bated breath for her to continue, but just like that she was done.

Not only had they received confirmation that Marigold had left without meeting Alberto, but someone matching Solei's description had followed Marigold out. That was a problem for their version of events: Solei didn't mention meeting Marigold. This new information complicated things. The case was more knotted than a rope on a naval ship.

Rose eyed Hamilton as they walked back to their vehicle. He thumbed through his notes as Hamilton got into the car with a grunt. She turned to him as they almost simultaneously exclaimed, "What the hell?!" They laughed, releasing the tension momentarily.

"Are you as excited, hopeful, confused, and irritated with the information we just received?" Hamilton asked, shaking her head.

"For lack of a better word—Dude."

"So, Quispe—Alberto, that is—was here, but didn't come inside. Solei was here, but failed to mention that she not only knew who Hunter was the whole time, but was possibly here and saw her father… and talked to Hunter. Oh, and she may have been here before." Hamilton said, catching her breath.

"Okay, that occurred to you, too. I thought maybe I was trying to connect dots that weren't there. Had Solei seen her father with Hunter at this café? What did Hunter tell us Solei said? Something to the effect of— 'he's not who you think.' How long between Alberto leaving and the two women departing?" Rose asked. They had so many half-answered and unanswered questions; it was turning into a tangled mess.

"In fairness, we had just notified the Quispes about Alberto's death. Everyone in that house acted off, and I mean, way off. That being said, I think we need to have a more in-depth chat with Solei. The mother, too. But based on the way she shut down during the notification, I'd prefer to give her a few days. Everyone we've met so far has a damn good motive. Everyone except Camila, but that woman is off, too."

"Um, let's go talk to Officer Simmons. See what Alberto's state of mind was… if anyone tailgated him, etcetera? Rose added. "Meanwhile, why don't you give Solei a call and see if we can schedule a time for her to come down to the station—alone."

***

As the detectives headed back to the precinct, Hamilton tried calling Solei, but it went to voicemail. She left a voicemail, letting Solei know they needed to speak again. They got lucky and caught Simmons just as he was about to head back out on patrol. He had noticed a white vehicle keeping pace with Quispe, but he didn't get the make and model. Officer Simmons offered that Alberto seemed jumpy and kept looking around as if he was followed, but tried hard to pretend he was nonchalant. Simmons had assumed Quispe was in a rush and embarrassed to have been pulled over. As the detectives walked back from Simmons' vehicle, Rose stopped mid-stride. "Shit! I'm pretty sure the make and model of the victim's vehicle has a LoJack on it."

"You're kidding! I'm realizing no one asked about his car during the notification. Guess we're going inside to get a warrant," Hamilton replied.

Chapter 26

Solei

Solei cursed as her call was sent to voicemail. She wondered what her friend was doing, but also understood that Camila may need a mental break from her family drama. Almost home, she told herself. Solei wanted to cry as the last few days settled in, but she was determined not to fall apart.

"Now is not the time to start being fragile," she said aloud. Her family deserved more than what the police seemed to be doing. She deserved more than half-truths and accusations. For the first time in a long time, she felt empowered to act, to be in possession of all the facts, despite how painful they might be.

Trying to take in the picture of fall outside her car window, Solei started a mental checklist. Wine. Desk. Agenda. She wanted to see if he'd written about her mother, and selfishly, about her. She was only sure of two things—she had to read through the entire thing tonight, maybe even take pictures, before she lost her nerve.

She needed to turn it over to the police. Her mother had already lied to them. Her best friend was involved in the car crash. No matter how minor her part was, it still looked extremely suspicious. Then, there was the fact that Camila was there when they made the notification. It was a nightmarish novella she wished she were watching from the outside.

"It's now or never," she told herself as she pulled up to her apartment. Solei closed her eyes, took a deep breath, then headed inside to face whatever waited. She wasted no time, afraid she would lose her nerve. Throwing her purse on the sofa, she headed directly to the kitchen for the bottle and her favorite "Eff the Patriarchy" wine glass. It felt like kismet that she still had some extra sharp cheddar in the fridge. Solei silently thanked God, then headed upstairs with her makeshift picnic. She nestled comfortably at her desk, taking a few swigs of wine and stuffing her face with cheese.

"I should light my candle," Solei said to no one as she rose to grab it. She made a production of looking for the Sea Spa scented wax and the grill lighter, sitting in their usual places. Her life had always been a struggle between pleasing her mother and trying to be nothing like her. She was failing at the latter. Still, Solei rummaged through random drawers, checked the kitchen pantry, and stood there with her hands on her hips, looking around, before returning to her bedroom and grabbing both the candle and lighter from her small bookshelf. She sat down and took another sip of wine and plopped cheese into her mouth.

"Just do it for God's sake," she said, exasperated at herself. As she lifted the agenda, she noticed that there were little scraps of paper hanging out of the edges of the book. Solei opened it and leafed through the pages, flipbook-style. There were pages crudely torn out. She dropped the book as if it were hot. Her eyes darted back and forth, feeling her anxiety rise like vomit through her belly and up to her throat. The tightness in her neck felt familiar, and she fought to stave off the paralysis that followed. Her mind delved into scenario after scenario of how and when the pages could have been ripped out, until finally her denial landed her exactly where she needed to keep her sanity.

"You've only read an entry or two… and you've only briefly flipped to this or that page," she said aloud. She tried to reinforce her version of reality where she simply missed the ripped pages the first few times she leafed through it. Solei blocked every scenario that funneled through her mind. "Hmm, where to start." She thought back to what she read last: *HIJA TIME*. She decided not to start there, but when she turned to that section to tab it with sticky notes, she noticed two of the section's pages were missing. Like a sudden high beam flash, she realized Luz hadn't mentioned her dad's agenda to the police. Solei knew what to search for next.

Solei flipped to the week they were supposed to have dinner, and the week of her father's supposed death. On that Sunday, she saw her father's handwriting: ~~Tell Solei?~~ It was scratched out. In the margin on the left, labeled *Notes*, he scribbled, "I miss my Solei."

Solei's stomach felt like a wiry ball. Though it was four words, it was something. For Solei, it was everything. A single teardrop splashed onto the page.

Solei's eyes were then drawn to angry red lettering in the box for Thursday. Alberto had written *Confront Luz*. Then, on Friday, *Tell Marigold*, and on Saturday, written with a small heart, *Tell Solei*.

Chapter 27

Marigold

The last few months flashed in rapid succession through Marigold's mind. With every memory came missed opportunities to steal a kiss, to let a touch linger between them. The platonic nature of their relationship loomed larger and larger in Marigold's imagination. She didn't want to believe that she had imagined it all, but if Alberto truly thought she was his daughter, he couldn't possibly have been trying to seduce her. Goosebumps formed on her arms and legs as she recalled the fantasies about them running away together, about him doting on her as they lived happily ever after. She only avoided gagging because her fantasies were intimate, not sexual.

With every clear thought, she felt more and more unhinged until the urge to run headfirst into a wall thrummed inside her. Intimate, not sexual, she thought again, soothing her mounting fear and will to self-harm. The first time she saw him, her inclination was to think of him as a cool friend of her father's. And it hit her like a bag of bricks—she had been so lonely. She felt lonely until this man came along to be in her space. Alberto made her feel less… invisible.

She had projected her need for a friend, her need to feel companionship, and that's what Alberto gave her. Tears mustered at the corners of Marigold's eyes. She missed him—the attention, the scandal, the excitement, them being each other's secret. And in a very different way, although they were each other's secret. He had a wife, a daughter, and she was his family, but not technically theirs. Had they known about her? Was Alberto her biological father? Marigold knew what it meant for her parents, for her father whom she loved dearly. And yet… she still wished Alberto was hers—in any way.

Something else peeked from the frightening corners of her mind… that morning, the dark reality of her reaction. And what of the night before? How else could he have gotten there? And why that feeling? The feeling of having lost time?

She felt herself—her mind—splintering, but a knock at her hospital room door boomeranged her back to alertness.

"Miss Hunter," the doctor said, drawing out the *Miss.* "I'd like to talk to you about your recent DNA test if you're up for it."

Marigold perked up at this, splashing her face one last time before coming out of the bathroom. She needed to know if Alberto was her father like she needed to bust out of that hospital.

The mere prospect changed everything, and something inside Marigold whispered a fear she couldn't face.

The whisper grew louder. *If he's your father, you know what that means.* Marigold physically shook her head to lose the thought.

"Please just tell me," she said, almost inaudibly.

"Ms. Hunter. The test was conclusive—Alberto Quispe is not your biological father. I have to tell you that the police are entitled to this information. You gave consent, so they do not need a warrant."

The doctor gave her a half-hearted smile.

Marigold knew it was meant to be reassuring, but nothing could do that at this point.

As he stood up to leave, he said, "And I'm not sure if you can withdraw consent."

Marigold understood, but she wanted the police to know Alberto wasn't her father. She wanted everyone to know she wasn't crazy—it hadn't been all in her head.

He thought he was your father… the whisper taunted.

"No, that's okay. I want them to know. Something tells me it might help. But Doc… is there an ETA on when I'll be discharged?" Marigold asked, hopeful. There was subtext behind her words.

He came back to her bedside, checking her heart rate and pupils, then her chart.

Finally, he said, "I'd like to keep you here for at least a few more days, but then I'm afraid your, uh, accommodations will no longer be up to either one of us."

Marigold nodded.

As Marigold sat in the cold, bright room alone, she began to weep. She had convinced herself that the results would make a difference, that they would matter, but what mattered was that Alberto thought he was her father.

She knew what that meant. Not for the first time, her feelings and experience had betrayed her. It had been years since she'd felt this way, since she'd started seeing the new psychiatrist, but once again, she couldn't trust herself.

Chapter 28

Hamilton

"Yes!" Rose exclaimed as he slammed his desk phone onto the receiver.

Hamilton looked at him, raising her eyebrows.

"We've got our warrant. Calling Crime Tech now," Rose added as he dialed the department's extension.

"Hi, Detective Rose. We need to track the LoJack on a vehicle with license plate number…" He shuffled through the mess of papers on his desk, searching for the details.

Hamilton had her own big piece of evidence. She sat back and studied her partner intently. As soon as he hung up the phone, she let out a low whistle just before he could dive back into the papers or make another call.

"Wanna guess what I have?" Hamilton smiled mischievously. She knew he hated being forced to guess.

He didn't answer; just gave her a look.

"Fine. DNA is in, and Quispe is not the father."

"You're frigging kidding me?! I swear, this case gets more and more bizarre with each new piece of info."

Rose sat back hard in his chair. "Food?"

Hamilton simply nodded.

***

Hamilton stared out the car window while Rose drove, watching the passersby, her gaze shifting subtly now and then. For a moment, everything they had learned about the case hung in the air between them, daring them to make it all fit.

Then Hamilton pulled out her notebook and turned toward her partner. She began reading aloud every note she had written. Rose nodded along in agreement.

Finally, he asked, "Why the hell does everyone believe Quispe is this woman's father? I mean, there's the letter, sure, but the family hasn't even produced it. Does it really exist?

"I mean, it has to exist, right? Quispe went there looking for Hunter for a reason. He spent time with her for a reason. This'll sound absolutely bonkers, but I'm starting to think Marigold is a pawn... but for who? And why lie about her being the love child—or the existence of one?"

Rose rubbed his hand down his face. "I'd say let's talk to Quispe's friends, find out if there ever was a mistress—but how do we even find those names?"

Chapter 29

Solei

"Mama, they're um... releasing dad's body tomorrow. Think you're up for that?" Solei asked, though she had wanted to be the one to do it. She was surprised her mother answered her call after the way they'd left things.

"What time, mi hija? I have so many things to do and…," Luz started to say, but Solei cut her off.

"Ta bien, Mama. I can sign for Papi's body. I have to go down there to answer more questions anyway. I'm kind of nervous," Solei replied. She was surprised her mother trusted her to handle so many of the logistics. The controlling maniac she knew had acted so differently over the last few weeks or so, but Solei knew this was a big deal. Still, she obliged.

"Why are they questioning *you?* They know it was *la hija de bruja*. He was in *her* trunk! Do not go down there without our lawyer," Luz demanded.

"Aye mami, esta bien. It's not like that. I don't need a lawyer," Solei replied, then tried to change the subject. "Isn't the appointment at the funeral parlor soon?"

Luz was not taking the bait. "*Mira tonta.* Do not go there without a lawyer. There's nothing you could tell them," Luz paused and took in a sharp breath. Then, she said, "Anyway, yes, it's soon. Now that we will have your father's body—God rest his soul—we can make official arrangements."

Solei made a mental note, then said, "Okay, Mama. Before you go—weird question—Papi's will?" She knew how it would look, her asking about the will, but she wanted her mother's reaction. She also needed to know if Marigold was in her father's will, and even more so, if her mother was in the possession of that knowledge. There would be a reading, but Solei needed to hear it from her mother before the formality of the lawyers and offices where Luz would, no doubt, exercise her perfect restraint.

At this point, Solei didn't care what her mother thought of her.

She registered the surprise in Luz's voice. Unlike her mother, she had never cared for material things. Luz had endured the mistresses and the lies, the long nights waiting up and the very early mornings serving him, pretending she wasn't the reason they were financially comfortable. And in true fashion, her father might give it away on a whim.

"Mama?" Solei asked.

"Don't be ridiculous, *niña.* We'll hear the will after your father's funeral as is appropriate. Now, are you coming or not?

The appointment is soon," Luz said, heading out of the door. "I can pick you up."

Solei knew better than to object.

***

Solei stood outside her townhouse apartment, palm burning with each scrape of her nails—nails that were, as her mother put it, "insufferably long." She suffered no delusion that her mother would take a break from the usual chastisement of her place. The gutters, the shutters, the porch—were all "despicable" and "unbecoming." The entire notion that she would live anywhere other than home until she was married was a "preposterous rebellion." *You're paying off mistresses*, Solei thought. The loud burst of her mother's car horn interrupted her anxiety cloud. Solei steadied herself with a deep breath.

The car ride was long and silent—Solei didn't have the emotional bandwidth to deal with her mother, and in such a small space. She guessed her mother's wheels were turning. Then, Luz peeked at her daughter so quickly she almost missed it. This was Luz's usual way of goading a conversation from Solei, but Solei simply smiled and pretended to get a text message.

The two spent the 20-minute car ride embroiled in their game of who would speak first. Solei was determined to win this game of chicken, despite the rising tension as they drew closer and closer to the funeral parlor.

When the two women arrived, Luz took a few minutes to check her makeup and smooth out her clothing. Solei let out a short but shrill "Ha," before fleeing the rigidity of the car. Luz simply shook her head incredulously, then gracefully stepped out herself.

As they strode into the parlor, Luz grabbed Solei's hand and gave it a slight squeeze. This small gesture was more than Solei could have expected, and just enough to keep her from breaking down. In that moment, Solei felt like her mother really saw her—even though she was still looking forward stoically. That small remembrance of Solei's anxiety surrounding anything funereal was a big deal for Luz.

The parlor was warmly lit with dark drapes drawn to let in the natural light. Though meant to be soothing, the pulsing trickle and swish of the zen water gardens made Solei's palms sweat. Her eyes darted from the dark drapes fluoresced by sunlight to the cherry wood, pine, and mahogany of the display caskets. The nightmarish maroon of the carpeting juxtaposed with the painted depictions of picnicking and revelry prickled at her. The finery of wallpaper, carpet, and caskets was just the kind of thing her mother loved. At one point, Luz even nodded in approval.

"Mrs. Quispe. I am so sorry for your loss. Oh, and this must be the darling Solei. Solei, dear, welcome. I'm Gerard McCafferty. Let's go into my office," the man said with a voice that had both a boom and a lilt. Solei and Luz followed as he walked, hands folded across his slightly protruding stomach, elbows tucked close to his sides. Something about a person walking without swinging their arms always rubbed Solei the wrong way.

The man swung to face them swiftly when he reached his desk, which startled Solei.

"So, tell me about your dear husband," he began. Luz proceeded to tell McCafferty about the loving family man and entrepreneur Alberto was, and how he came to a tragic demise.

Solei simply sat there in a fog of anxiety. She didn't have her usual safety net of escape. She had mostly drowned out her mother's clearly rehearsed story. And even though Luz had not seen Alberto in his new state, she promptly sourced it as the reason for wanting a cremation.

"I'm sorry—what?" Solei asked, nearly choking on her surprise.

"I said we want a cremation," Luz repeated matter-of-factly.

"Mama, Papi would not want a cremation. I know that for a fact."

"I'll give you two a moment alone to discuss," the man said. Before he could leave the room, their voices were already rising.

"Who do you think you are telling me what my husband would have wanted? Your attitude and disrespect have been out of control lately. Now, I'll cut you some slack because you're going through something, *pero cuidado*," Luz said.

She paused and smoothed out her perfect clothing, then told Solei in Spanish not to question her ever again, especially in public or in front of other people. Then, Luz took a deep breath, and beckoned the funeral director to return.

Solei seethed. If she had not ridden with her mother to the parlor, and wasn't scared to defy her again openly, she would have stormed out. Instead, she sat there with her arms crossed, breath and anger turbulent in her chest, trying to regulate her breathing. Her thoughts were a frenzy with ways she could keep her mother from cremating her father. Part of her frenzy came from feeling she didn't have any recourse—her mother was the next of kin and official word on his funeral rights. Her father would not want a cremation.

She studied her mother as Luz talked with a deliberate amount of grief, and a small smile that imbued the perfect percentage of *I'm suffering, but with grace.*

Solei wondered if her mother truly cared about what condition her father may be in for an open casket—whether that was for Luz's own sanity or for the feelings of those who might attend the funeral—or if it were something more sinister. Did her mother need so badly to have the last vengeful word, or was she covering something else up? Solei expelled the thought from her head. She didn't want to believe her mother went so far as to take her father away from her, but she also tried to convince herself that the autopsy would have already discovered anything a cremation could cover up. Finally, Solei decided her mother was simply being true to her nature. *Controlling even in death, Mama.*

Chapter 30

Hamilton

"Quispe's car is located on West Chestnut Street behind General Hospital," Rose said.

Hamilton had other ideas as she sped past Exit 3, making a beeline for downtown Wilkes-Barre.

"And how long will it take officers to get on the scene? Okay, we'll be there shortly. Make sure the scene is absolutely secure. We've most likely lost a lot of evidence based on time alone," Rose instructed before clicking his screen off.

Before Hamilton could say anything, Rose was already calling the pizzeria to order their slices. She looked at him with a wide grin.

Within 20 minutes, they had picked up their food and arrived at the site. The crime scene technicians and officers had cordoned off the area, but Hamilton noticed that there were hard brake tracks burned into the road at the top of the block.

She pulled past the turn onto West Chestnut and put on her hazards. Then, she hailed one of the officers, asking him to get a roadblock started for the entire one block, pointing out the tracks. He cast his eyes downward, and barked orders over the radio. A crime scene technician or CST quickly came over and began to measure and photograph the tracks extensively.

Careful not to trample any evidence, the detectives passed the cordon and approached the senior technician, Gilbert Monroe.

"Rosey," Monroe exclaimed upon seeing the detectives. He elbow-bumped Rose and gave him a playful smile before nodding at Hamilton.

"Hello to you, too, Gilbert," Hamilton retorted.

Rose laughed.

Hamilton and Monroe exchanged obligatory half-smiles, then Hamilton continued, "Anything so far?"

"A little and a lot. Based on what we know so far, I'd lean towards a hit-and-run. The car door was slightly ajar, the keys were found over yonder in some weeds, and there's tire tracks, which I pointed out to the officers on the scene, but were subsequently ignored. That looks as if someone sped up, but then came to a hard stop shortly after the possible hit," Monroe summarized.

"Oh, and there's also blood along the side of his back and driver's door. Someone wiped it, but the luminol proves its presence."

Hamilton and Rose exchanged glances.

"And inside the car?" Hamilton asked.

"Nothing too out of the ordinary, but we did find something in the glove compartment," Monroe replied as he pulled out a transparent bag of evidence. Rose grabbed it, almost snatching it from his friend's hand, and flipped it over. On the back of the photo, written in neat handwriting, were the words, "Our daughter, our Marigold," followed by an address and phone number.

Thinking the address sounded familiar, Hamilton pulled out her phone and plugged it into Google Maps. The location emerged as the *Tea, Read, Love Café*, Marigold's place of employment. Hamilton flipped open her phone and showed Rose. The two stood there, staring at each other.

Hamilton opened the camera application on her phone, snapping a photo of the front and back of the evidence. Chain of custody had to be preserved. Rose nodded to his partner, who immediately thanked Monroe, then started walking out of earshot of everyone on the scene. Hamilton studied the photo on her phone, then looked at her partner. She didn't know where to start.

"So… we really need to check both Marigold's car again and her alibi. It's possible she followed him after leaving the café, hit him with her car, and dragged his body into the trunk, but witnesses say he left several minutes before she did. How could she have known where he went, let alone catch up to him? And then, this photo…" Rose trailed off. He bit his lip.

"This has to be the photo that was in the letter, yet this is clearly taken from afar," Hamilton said.

"That ain't no family photo. Definitely taken from afar. Honestly, that alone is enough to make me question both the intentions of the letter sender and Marigold's culpability. Alberto should have noticed the oddity of the picture, too. At the same time, he'd just been told both that he had a love child and that his wife had paid the mother to disappear." Rose said.

"And why give her work address rather than home? We know Alberto was not Marigold's father, but should we assume Marigold's mother didn't send that letter? Also, except for there being a mistress, and the wife paying her off, the information could have been gleaned with very little effort. Who wrote the damn letter, because if they aren't the killer, they're at the very least culpable of something… I don't know what exactly, but something." Hamilton was miffed.

"It's still highly possible that someone wrote that letter for nefarious reasons, and the revelation—or Alberto not leaving his wife like she thought he would—made Hunter snap. Who knows if she meant to make it out of that accident? What's more, if she did hit him with her car, the accident could have been a cover-up."

"I mean, why write the letter? To embarrass Quispe? To extort him?" Hamilton felt like she was onto something. Blackmail, wills, money, in general, were the greatest motives of all, next to a crime of passion.

"But where do we start?" Rose asked.

"With Marigold. Honestly, she's the only one we haven't caught in an outright lie thus far. Also, nothing you mentioned is out of the realm of possibility," Hamilton admitted.

"She seems just as confused as us," Rose snorted.

"Back to basics then, I guess. Let's go ask her about her alibi, ask her about this photograph, too," Hamilton continued. "Maybe even ask her about her enemies."

Solei

On the way back to her apartment, Solei watched the clock. She counted trees outside the window, checked social media. Solei could feel her mother's eyes on her like daggers at every red light and stop sign.

She opened her messaging application and sent a text to Camila—*SOS. IFC. Meet at my place in a half hour?*

Solei watched intently as the three dots bounced, signaling Camila's reply. Her fingernails dug into the phone with anticipation until *See you soon* popped onto the screen. Solei let out the breath she didn't realize she was holding in. She felt better about the prospect of wine and conversing with her best friend, but the tension of being in the car with her mother was still visceral.

"*Soy tu madre.* You can't ignore me forever," Luz finally said, breaking the silence.

More like the evil stepmother, Solei thought to herself, giving her mother a half-hearted smile. Then she studied her mother sitting there, perfectly poised, nonplussed by the fact that she was ignoring her husband's last wishes. The smallest thing was ignited in Solei—not hate. Solei loved her mother, but something close to it. She ruminated and landed on exactly what it was. She had finally lost the last bit of respect for her.

Solei kissed her mother on the cheek and whispered her *bendición* when they arrived at her place. The cool air of the early evening filled her as the vacuum of tension released its hold on her lungs. More and more, Solei found that she had to remind herself to breathe when around Luz. The more lies that came to light, the more Solei felt she didn't know her mother—not really. She always knew her mother could be cold, controlling, and manipulative, but she thought it was a combination of her fear and love. Now, Solei was beginning to think her mother's actions were pure self-preservation.

How far would you go, Mama? she thought before stepping onto her porch.

As Solei waited for Camila to arrive, she opened a bottle of their favorite wine and laid out some veggie baked crackers, hard salami, and various cheeses. This wouldn't be their typical girls' night; Solei needed a reprieve. Everything she'd known felt as if it were crumbling in her hands. The more she tried to keep hold, the faster the crumble. If she was going to spiral, a little charcuterie was the least she deserved. She couldn't really process her father's death until she solved his murder… or the police did.

There was a soft rap at her door.

"Coming," Solei said.

Camila stepped inside and gave Solei a hug. A smile opened broadly across her face as her eyes landed on the spread.

"Thank God for you," Camila exclaimed, popping off her shoes and plopping down onto the sofa. "You literally read my soul. Let's have a few drinks before we dive in."

The two broke into brief, scattered bursts of laughter as they sat, sipping wine and picking at their snacks. Finally, Solei put her wine glass down on the koa table, leaned back, and closed her eyes. She took a deep breath and, even with her eyes closed, could feel her friend staring at her.

They exchanged knowing sighs before Camila finally said, "*Dímelo.*"

"I finally looked through the entire thing—my father's agenda, I mean. Well, I read the parts that were still in there," Solei said, looking down at what was left of the cheese and crackers.

Camila's eyes grew wide.

"What do you mean 'parts that were still there?'" Camila asked.

"Some of the pages were ripped out. I almost had a full panic attack but managed to calm myself. I could have just missed that the first time, right? The important thing is that I finally forced myself to look through the entire thing and I'm really glad I did," Solei said.

Camila nodded.

"I think my father was tormented by it all, but he did plan on telling me and…" Solei's voice trailed off.

Solei knew what she wanted to say, the thing that would make it more real than she could handle. So, she said the closest thing she could to it.

"In my father's last entry, on the day he died, he had written, 'Confront Luz.' Do you think that's… ominous?" Solei stopped herself from continuing, then tucked her palms under her thighs. She refused to let the scratching start.

Then, Solei continued, "And you'll never guess what my darling Mama decided today. She's getting my father cremated. Can you freaking believe her? My father would never want to be cremated."

Solei paused, hoping that for once her friend would let the conversation stay on this new trajectory. She said what she could, and for the moment, needed to leave it there.

Camila, however, had a look on her face that frightened Solei. Solei didn't dare say another word, instead waited for Camila to push further. Her heartbeat seemed to foxtrot.

Finally, Camila asked, "Have you asked Luz where she was Friday night?"

Chapter 31

Marigold

Marigold brushed her unruly hair as Detective Hamilton and Rose entered her room. Her nose had been wiped raw, and dry tears streaked her cheeks.

"I told you he wasn't my father," she said, repeatedly rolling her hands around her wrists. Over the past few days, anxiety and loneliness had settled in as she learned that she had been completely wrong about her relationship with Alberto.

A part of her wanted to tell the detectives more about the body. She didn't think she had any real reason to murder Alberto, but the body had been in her home.

Marigold wanted to yell it at top volume, to tell them that she had transported his body, but that she didn't *think* she killed him. *How do you tell the police that you don't think you killed someone?*

"Please don't look at me like that," Marigold said, recognizing a look of pity on Hamilton's face. "I want to know what's going on too."

Hamilton nodded. "Right. Where were you Friday evening through Saturday morning before the accident? Specifically, when did you leave the café, and where did you go and/or what did you do?" Hamilton asked, having her notepad in hand.

"After I saw Alberto pull away, I tried to call him and left. I sent a not-so-nice voicemail, then sent him some follow-up text messages of equal... disdain. A few short minutes later, I walked out of the café. Oh—shortly before that—is when I ran into his daughter, or at least whom I presumed to be her. She told me Alberto was not who I thought he was. I asked her if she was his daughter, but her response was 'it doesn't matter.'

"I felt bad, ya know. For breaking up their family, for getting mad at Alberto for leaving when, of course, he couldn't have stayed with his daughter there.

"I was pissed and sad, and I... I just needed to talk to my mother, okay?" Marigold's voice cracked.

"I do that, ya know—go and talk to her. It used to be that I only went to see her when I was going through something. Ya know, a girl needs her mother. For the past few months... I guess I just decided why shouldn't I get to see her— figuratively speaking—whenever I want."

Marigold noticed the looks of utter confusion on both Hamilton and Rose's faces. She then clarified herself. "My mother's dead—just over one and a half years now. I visit with her at St. Vicente Cemetery.

"Anyway, after that I went to Redleaf, then home to eat and polished off a bottle of Pinot." The last part was made up. The truth was Marigold didn't remember exactly what she did after Redleaf.

"In the morning—" she continued. "I was on my way to run some errands before therapy when I got into the accident."

"I am very sorry to hear about your mother's passing. I can imagine that was very hard for you. Do you know about what time you arrived at the cemetery? Do you have a receipt from Redleaf?" Hamilton asked evenly.

"I don't… know what time I arrived. But! But I had to call the groundskeeper to let me into the cemetery. I'm sure he can remember letting me in… or, can you check my phone records or something? See that I made the call, what time, maybe even that I made it from the grounds of the cemetery? Right? Please say you can," Marigold pleaded.

She made sure to meet Hamilton's eyes with her own, then Rose's. She needed someone to believe her, to help her, because she could do neither for herself.

"Oh, and if my wallet was found in the accident, or my cell phone, you can check for the Redleaf receipt and even my banking app to see the date and time of the charge. Right?" Marigold asked, looking back and forth between the detectives who were furiously taking notes.

The young woman's desperation hung between them all.

Hamilton looked her in the eyes and said, "We will check the phone records and confirm your alibi."

"Yes, I give you my permission," Marigold said eagerly.

There was a risk of the detectives finding something incriminating, but she herself needed to know. From one moment to the next, she questioned her propensity for murder, and it scared her to her depths.

The detectives kept exchanging glances that made her nervous, but there was something about this interview versus the last. This time, she sensed that the detectives believed her.

Suddenly, Hamilton reached into her pocket. Marigold winced. Hamilton pulled out her phone and tapped away. Then, she showed Marigold the screen. "Do you recognize this picture?"

Marigold stared at it; eyebrows screwed together. She thought hard about it, then her brain clicked.

"Yes, actually. I vaguely remember a friend snapping that picture of me. Only because of the blue jean jacket and white sundress I'm wearing in it. The dress was ruined, and I cried for hours because it was my mother's. A friend of mine took that picture at a fair at Kirby Park. I had started to walk off to grab something to eat, I think. She posted it to Instagram forever ago.

"Why do you have it?" Marigold couldn't think of a reason they would or could have the photo.

"Mr. Quispe received this photograph. This may be why he was under the impression that you're his long-lost child," Hamilton said.

Rose searched Marigold's face for a reaction. Something was off.

Marigold began to cry. She wept for Alberto, and for herself.

"Ms. Hunter, we'll check the phone records—" Rose began. "This way we can check on your alibi… maybe… clear your name?"

Marigold nodded as Rose jotted everything into his notepad. Hamilton nodded in his direction, then turned back to Marigold with a smile.

"Ms. Hunter, we'll take our leave now. Once the doctors clear you, you will be moved to a correctional facility. I highly recommend you get yourself a good lawyer… right away," Hamilton said.

Solei

The dim lighting of Solei's living room aligned with the malaise of the silence she now shared with her best friend. Solei stared blankly at Camila for several seconds, making her second guess what she said. Finally, Solei blinked and took her phone out. "What… are you doing?" Camila asked, concern riddling her face.

"I don't know," Solei replied, sloshing her words ever so slightly. Her phone rang. Solei had dialed Luz and put her on speaker.

"Haylo…" Luz said. "You ready to apologize to your mother?" she continued, less asking, more demanding.

"Mama, why are you doing this?" Solei asked, her voice cracking. "Papi would not want to be cremated, and you know that. Please just be honest with me."

Luz sighed heavily on the other end. "Aye, *mi hija*. Did you ever stop to think about my feelings? How his death has affected me? Do you think I want to see your father like that? Who knows what that *loca* did to him… *por Dios*, he was in her trunk," Luz's voice trailed off.

Even in her drunkenness, Solei felt a tinge of regret at questioning her mother. There were still unanswered questions and her mother's questionable behavior. Solei, however, had no intention of hurting her mother. She had been through enough.

"I'm going tomorrow to sign for his release. I can let you know… um, if he's not too bad. I just feel like you'll regret not seeing him at least one last time," Solei said. She remembered why she called in the first place.

"Mama, when was the last time you saw Papi?" Solei asked, with real concern though she had an ulterior motive.

Luz sighed again, "Friday, okay! You happy now? I saw your father on Friday. And we had an argument, so don't go running your mouth to the police about this."

"Mama! Don't say that…" Solei trailed off. She wanted to know more, to ask what they argued about, but she couldn't alienate her mother now. Luz was all she had left, and it made her feel every emotion. She didn't want to need her mother.

"We argued because he was upset. He was upset that I knew about Marigold, and that I paid that woman, River, to go away. Of course, it didn't matter that she was quick to take the money. It didn't even occur to him the pain I must have felt about him stepping out on me and fathering a *pinche* child.

"We argued, and he stormed out… to see her, his bas— his extramarital child. He told me he was going to meet her somewhere to tell her that he's her father," Luz admitted. "That's it. Okay, last I saw he was driving away to see her. Then, she killed him! So, stop questioning every damn thing I do."

Solei looked at her friend, intending to roll her eyes, but Camila had a look on her face that scared some of the drunk off of her.

"What?" Solei mouthed.

Camila simply shook her head, but Solei felt she had more to say. "*Perdón*, Mama. I love you. Talk tomorrow?" Solei asked. "Mama?" Solei asked again.

"Talk tomorrow, *mi hija. Te amo*," Luz said, with a loud exhale, then hung up.

"Okay, so what was that look about? There were figurative daggers coming out of your eyes. Please—I just can't take any more lies and half-truths," Solei pleaded.

"There's no easy or nice way to say this. So, I'm just going to say it and you can do with it, what you will," Camila admitted, then word vomited the rest. "Luz just lied to you.

"Friday, I drove past that café… and your mother and father were both there. It really only stuck with me because I thought it was weird that they were in separate cars. If he stormed out to meet with that woman like Luz said, then your mother definitely had to have followed him there."

Chapter 32

Solei

It's your husband's funeral, for Pete's sake. No one is expecting you to be perfect, Mama, Solei thought. Her mother flitted around their home, tidying already spotless surfaces, checking on the perfect spread of food and charcuterie, and swimmingly performing the role of sad but gracious hostess.

"Mama, is there anything I can do?" Solei asked, smiling. She gently grabbed her mother by the shoulders to get her attention, staring directly into Luz's eyes. She was trying to discern what her mother was going through—trying to detect some visceral emotion. There was the flicker of something, but the doorbell rang before either could respond.

"Ay, they're here," Luz yelped. She gave her daughter a quick, but tight hug, then rushed to get the door. Luz was a stickler for being the perfect hostess, even in times like these. She never let someone—especially family—wait at the door too long. She gestured for Solei to come stand by her side.

One by one, each family member drifted past them in the foyer and through to the kitchen, each receiving *bendiciones* and cheek kisses in response to their condolences. Each stopped to admire the large photograph of Alberto that sat on an easel by the mantel of the fireplace. Next to the easel was a table with a beautiful and intricate white lace doily, with Alberto's gold and blue urn sitting atop it.

As more of Alberto's family members arrived, the room seemed to grow warmer, and everyone present started to move into their own silos. Whispers, looks, and fake smiles abounded. Solei simply let her eyes float from one group to the next, astonished at each part of her family's inability to truly be there for one another. She felt the sting of every smile shot at her mother. Everyone seemed to show genuine compassion towards Solei, but it wasn't enough. The entire funeral felt like a farce, and she thought her father deserved more. With each moment that passed, her anxiety turned to anger. When she finally felt like she'd explode, her mother stood and cleared her throat.

Between light sobs and nose blows into a handkerchief, Luz began a prayer, then asked anyone who wanted to come up to say a few words. Solei's *tíos* came up, one by one, to tell funny, heartfelt stories about their childhood with Alberto. His godbrother also came up to talk about Alberto's mischievous boyhood, and then his almost instant success with the family perfume shops. At this, Luz smiled the biggest, her face lighting up. Solei read her mother like a book; she was proud of her husband's business. Luz treated the business like their baby—their pride and joy. Solei always joked that she was her father's favorite child, and the business was her mother's.

When the fake compassion, stories of love, and good eats were done, folks began to somberly file out of the house. Three hours of this ordeal and the reading of the will to go, Solei thought. She didn't stand by the door to say goodbye to everyone—there was enough of that today. Instead, Solei stood by her father's urn, silently praying for his soul. A tear fell from each eye. She wiped them away, then whispered, "*Te amo, papi*. I'll figure it out. *Te prometo*."

"*Mi amor*, you ready to go?" Luz asked, squeezing her daughter's shoulder.

"Do we have to do this today?" Solei asked. "I just want to be with Papi."

"Didn't you just ask me about the will?" Luz replied callously, then muttered something under her breath.

Solei couldn't make it all out, but thought she heard Marigold's name. It only took an instant for her to decide that she didn't want to know. All of this was making her feel miserable and insane. Her mother insisted that they ride together to the lawyer's office, but Solei knew better. Her mother's request made it clear to her—what had her so nervous throughout the entire funereal process.

The toxicity of the room made her feel... trapped, and there was so much of that over the last few weeks. She was trapped in this limbo of finding out her parents' secrets and not being able to confront them, of her father avoiding her while he got to know a half-sister who neither of them had known existed. Solei was trapped between wanting to find justice for her father, but not wanting to lose another family member to do so. She needed a moment to explode. The pent-up energy threatened to consume her altogether, and she knew there was only one way to let it all out without hurting or scaring anyone.

After convincing her mother, Solei swiftly moved to her car. She sat in her car, waiting, nails scraping against her palms. When her mother finally pulled out of the driveway, she let out a scream that made the hair on her own arms stand at attention. Then she hissed as a drop of blood escaped from her palm.

***

Solei pulled into the parking lot to see Luz standing in front of the lawyer's office, arms crossed over her chest and her foot tapping. As soon as Luz saw the car, she threw her arms up dramatically—her mouth moving, no doubt whispering Spanish obscenities about Solei's tardiness.

Pulling a napkin from the glove compartment, Solei dabbed her face then palm before her mother could see she was crying. Solei took a deep breath, plastered on a warm smile, then opened the door to her mother's scolding.

"Perdón, Mamá, I had to run back in to use the bathroom," she said, the only excuse she could muster.

Luz just stood there, staring at her, then gestured for them to head inside.

Solei and Luz were escorted by the secretary into the cushy office. A large, high-end table with clawed feet stood in the middle of the warmly lit room. Seven leather-tufted chairs were pushed under the table. Her parents' lawyer stood from the chair at the head of the table as Solei and Luz entered the room. The man gave her mother a hug that lingered an awkward second longer than Solei cared for.

"I'm so sorry for your loss, Solei. Your father was a good man," he said, tone flat and monotonous.

"Thanks," Solei replied, more to appease her mother than in appreciation.

"Alright. Alberto wanted this to be very informal. He wrote a letter that he wanted me to read," he said before reading aloud.

> *To Mis Corazones,*
>
> *If you're hearing this, I have been taken from this world. Perdóname for leaving you. You two are the loves of my life. To my beloved Luz, I leave my sincerest apologies for everything that I put you through. You were the driving force of everything good in our lives. I leave you our businesses, in whole, and one-third of the sum of all of our assets minus what Mr. Vasquez has been instructed to donate. To my Solei, my sun and moon, I leave you the house—though I trust you will let your mother reside there until it's her time to join me—my car, and one-third of the sum of all my assets. There is also a sum of $100,000 for any further schooling and/or research.*
>
> *This part is very hard for me to write, but I feel it is the only fair outcome. First, Luz, I forgive you for keeping Marigold from me. I hate that you felt you had to do that, but I know I am partially to blame. Solei, I am sorriest to you for breaking your trust. Lastly, pending a positive paternity test, I leave the third sum of all my assets to my second-born daughter, Marigold Hunter.*
>
> *—Alberto*

Before Mr. Vasquez could finish reading Marigold's last name, Luz stood up so abruptly that her chair screeched.

"*Maldita*—" she began to yell when Solei gasped.

"Mami, please. *Cálmate, por favor*," Solei began, but Luz shot her a look of daggers. Solei's mouth shut abruptly, out of pure fear. She was likewise upset over this revelation, but hadn't expected her mother's reaction.

"Forty years I put into our marriage. You don't know what I had to give up… the things I had to endure. And now my daughter, our daughter has to share our family's wealth with some *pinche* bastard whose mother couldn't—"

"Mama, stop it! If she's his ch–" Suddenly, Solei felt the sting of Luz's hand whip across her face.

Both women stood there stunned into silence, staring at each other. Luz's eyes were still ablaze. Solei held back tears, the moment replaying in her mind.

Then, Luz tugged at the bottom hem of her blazer, took a deep breath, and turned to the lawyer. "That girl will get our family's money over my dead *pinche* body!" she said forcefully into Vasquez's face, then stormed out.

Solei stood there, silent, frozen, and mortified. No words could escape her mouth though she felt compelled to apologize for the scene her mother had made. Instead, Solei gulped down air, stood up, and turned on her heels, making a beeline for the exit.

Rose

Rose studied the plain, brown one-story building as he and his partner stepped out of the vehicle. Except for a small sign at the entrance of the parking lot, some shrubbery, and an even smaller golden placard on the front wall of the building, there was not much to the counseling office.

He said a silent prayer for someone in this place to at least acknowledge that Hunter used their services. Rose looked over at Hamilton, and she too looked pensive and unimpressed. Both smiled as their eyes met.

"Here goes nothing," Rose said.

Grateful that the place was empty, the two approached the receptionist's desk.

"Hi. I'm Detective Hamilton; this is my partner, Rose. We're investigating a murder. We need to speak with Marigold Hunter's doctor," Hamilton said with a smile.

The receptionist looked at her skeptically, taking both detectives in.

Hamilton added, "Ms. Hunter gave us this office as the location of her therapy services, but was… incapacitated before she had the chance to tell us the doctor's name."

"I feel like you know that I'm not allowed to say," the young woman said.

"I understand, I really do, about patient confidentiality. And I'm not asking you to tell us anything personal. I just want to know who she was seeing so we can ask a few follow-up questions—that's it. I'm trying to save Hunter from being charged with a crime she may not have committed," Hamilton responded.

She scrutinized Hamilton, then her face softened.

"I can't tell you that Marigold Hunter is a patient here, but I will page Dr. Walker for you," she replied, a glint in her eyes. She picked up the phone and pressed a few buttons. "There are detectives here to speak to you about a patient," she said into the receiver.

The door to the right of the desk buzzed, and a short, balding man in a polo, cardigan, and khakis came out to greet the detectives. He seemed a bit agitated, shooting the receptionist a look of disappointment as he beckoned them to follow him back to his office.

As they entered Walker's office, the cliché reverberated. The room was well-lit with warm-bulbed lamps, soothing music played, and there was the lightest drizzle and trickle of a tabletop rock fountain. Rose struggled to keep from audibly scoffing before asking Walker to turn off the music. For some reason, it made him uncomfortable.

"So, how can I help you? And before you ask, I cannot divulge anything that breaches doctor-patient confidentiality," he said matter-of-factly.

"We already know that you were treating Ms. Hunter. And we're not looking for anything personal here. We just need to verify whether she was here for an appointment on Saturday morning and if you think she is a danger to herself or anyone," Rose said impatiently.

The doctor sighed heavily and seemed to think for a second. Then, he looked away.

"Again, we're just looking to establish Hunter's whereabouts on the morning of Saturday, September 10. That's all. She told us she was here, and we just want to confirm. Even if it's just a head nod."

The doctor sat up and folded his hands on his desk. "Yes, she was here late Saturday morning. I'm afraid that is all I can say."

"And what of any danger?" Hamilton asked.

When he didn't respond, she said, "Dr. Walker, we

won't take up too much more of your time, and I respect the importance of confidentiality. You are, however, obligated to report patients that pose a danger to the public, so if you're holding anything back, you might face charges yourself."

Rose looked at her, surprised at her rash assertion. It wasn't like his partner. The doctor just sat there, mouth agape. Then he closed his mouth and stumbled to say something.

"Ms. Hunter is a danger to no one. I know what they're saying on the news, but I find it very hard to believe."

Rose didn't put it past anyone to do another harm. He hadn't ruled out the possibility that Hunter might have simply been a pawn or an accomplice, but her cemetary alibi with the groundskeeper did check out.

"Anyway, from my time with her—" Dr. Walker continued, crossing his arms over his protruding belly, "she presents as a timid, caring young lady who has simply struggled with some family issues. A bit imaginative, but not dangerous. And that's all I'm going to say without a subpoena."

Hamilton looked at him with unblinking eyes. "Thank you for your time, Dr. Walker," Hamilton replied. She looked at Rose and nodded.

The two stood to leave, the music starting up again as they exited the room.

Chapter 33

Hamilton

On their way back to the precinct, Hamilton's phone rang. "Please tell me you have something from the envelope."

"We sure do. Be back soon?" The forensics technician asked.

"Be down as soon as we get in," Hamilton replied. She had to smile as her partner rubbed his fingers into his temples. He looked ragged and pensive. "So?" she asked.

"What was that about back there? With the doc? You—you pulled a me," Rose said, chuckling.

"Honestly, I don't know. I've just had enough of it all. Every time I think we have something; some other truth comes to light. The woman had the damn body in her trunk for effs sake, and she has a history—this should have been open and shut. I don't know. Maybe she just has the worst luck in the world," Hamilton said.

"Welcome to my cynical world. Well, let's hope forensics isn't pulling our leg." Rose rolled his neck and stared out of the window. "What did they say?"

"Tech said they have something. Now, let's hope it isn't another wrench." Hamilton said.

The detectives went straight to the basement where forensics was housed. Both felt an urgency to see where this new evidence might set them back or catapult their case. Rose stood there, rubbing and rolling his neck. Finally, one of the technicians waved them over.

"Am I going to thank you or hate you for this?" Hamilton asked the technician.

"A little of both—maybe," the tech replied, flinching. "The good and bad news is that it wasn't mailed."

"Good and bad, huh? We really just need the nitty gritty here," Rose said.

The technician grimaced at Rose before he continued, "Bad because we don't have a clue about where the letter originated—what post offices it may have been routed through, etcetera. Good because that means that it was likely given directly to the victim—that reduces the chances of having a million and one fingerprints or DNA traces; it could have been contaminated going through the postal service. Now, here's where you'll thank me. Someone licked it, and… we have D… N… A."

"You're freaking kidding," Hamilton said, smiling and tapping the technician on the shoulder.

"We have DNA from the saliva of one person," he continued, snapping his fingers with delight. "We don't know who it belongs to, but we know who it doesn't belong to. It isn't the victim's or anyone related to him. And we have three sets of fingerprints—the victim's along with two others."

At this point, Rose was openly grinning, but Hamilton pressed her lips together. She couldn't bring herself to be as optimistic as her partner. There was still the collection of fingerprints and DNA, and that would require warrants.

They didn't have enough on Solei to request a warrant for her fingerprints, especially because it wasn't her DNA on that envelope. And the DNA and fingerprints weren't Hunter's or else the technician would have said so. Too many thoughts floated and bumped around in Hamilton's head. She needed to write it all down, take a deep breath, then look at each piece in this befuddled case. Her phone chimed, notifying her via email that she had a new voicemail.

"We'll get you that match," Hamilton said to the technician, then nodding to her partner as the two headed upstairs.

"What's up?" Rose inquired.

"Voicemail—at my desk. And anyway, I needed to get out of there. We have all the pieces, well almost, but I need a bird's eye view," Hamilton said to her partner.

"Got it. Check your voicemail. I'll get everything on the board," Rose replied.

As Hamilton dialed her voicemail, Rose began adding the new information in small bites to the clean marker board. Hamilton rummaged through her pockets, fingered through her notepad, jotted something down, then held it up for her partner to see. SOLEI was written in all caps. Rose looked at her quizzically. He scribbled faster. Taking a step back, he peeked at the notecards on the board, then moved them around again and again. When he turned, seemingly to ask Hamilton something, she was already dialing someone.

"Hi, Solci. How are you doing? Meet in person? Yes, I can… oh, you're here. I'll be down." Hamilton nodded towards the hall. "Room 1," she whispered to Rose.

***

When Hamilton saw Solei, her face was grief-stricken and her complexion clammy. The young lady seemed to falter in her step when she saw Hamilton. The detective felt a twinge of nervousness at the sight of her, clutching her purse like a bank robber. *She isn't stupid enough, right?* Hamilton thought to herself as Solei stepped through the metal detector. No beeps or whirs. Hamilton shook her head at her overreaction.

"I'm glad you're here," Hamilton said, smiling.

"I just—things have been happening. And… I really don't want to be here, but I can't deal—" Solei admitted, her eyes downcast as they entered the elevator.

Hamilton's heart began to race. *Is she here to confess?* She wasn't sure she truly saw Solei as a suspect. There *was* the café. Marigold said she spoke with Alberto's daughter, and there were witnesses. Hamilton made a mental note to show a photo of Solei to the café workers… and to Marigold.

Rose was already inside of the room, but Hamilton eyed him briefly. She wanted to take the lead. "Can I bring you anything, Ms. Quispe?" he asked, standing up and smiling as he walked out of the room.

Hamilton gestured for Solei to have a seat at the cold, metal table. She looked around nervously, still clutching her bag. "I… I don't want to be here. Did I say that already?"

Solei said, laughing nervously.

"I think that means you know you should be here. That's a pretty admirable quality, you know… doing what's right even when you don't want to," Hamilton replied with a warm smile.

"We buried… well—cremated my father. Had the funeral…" Solei trailed off, stifling tears. Sweat began to pool on her upper lip. She hissed as the sweat graced the open scratches. "I found this," Solei blurted out as she reached into her purse and dropped the agenda onto the table. "It's my father's agenda. I found it when I was helping my mother prepare for the funeral. I looked it over and—" Solei lurched forward abruptly.

Hamilton gave her the emotional space to gather her thoughts. This wasn't going in the direction she thought. Instead of prying, she nodded to her partner through the two-way glass. Rose was already grabbing an evidence bag and gloves. Slipping the evidence gear to his partner, Rose placed a cup of water close to Solei.

Hamilton donned a pair of latex gloves and placed the journal in the evidence bag.

"Check out the tabbed pages. I… I think my mother killed my father," she blurted, hand following in a frantic trail towards her mouth as though to stop the words from tumbling out. It was too late.

Rose and Hamilton's eyes snapped up in unison. Though neither knew what to expect, a finger of blame in the mother's direction was far from their minds. Neither detective said a word. Solei looked at the detectives as though trying to discern if they believed her or not. "Okay, um, so my mother has been acting very odd. You have to understand, my mother is a Type

A person. She needs to control… Well, everything. When you first told us of my father's passing, the mother I know would have asked a million questions; she would have been a bit hoity-toity with you two. Anyway, more than that, my father had plans to tell her about meeting with Marigold, and on the day before he was killed—" Solei paused.

"I feel like you have more to tell us, Solei," Hamilton pushed. Then, she reached over and gently squeezed Solei's hand.

"I—um—there's a will. Marigold was written in, well, pending a paternity test. I didn't know, but I don't see any reality where my mother didn't know about the will changes. She runs our family. I don't really care so much so long as Marigold didn't kill our father, but my mother would never go for it. She'll never say it because it's not proper, but my mother is the reason my father is so successful. In her mind, she built our family up and someone she sees as an… outsider is not entitled to that fortune. She made… a scene at the lawyer's office. And… she lied… I love my mother. I don't want it to be her. I just… she lied. Why would she lie?" Solei asked, another flood of tears staining her face.

"What did she lie about, Solei?" Hamilton asked gently. She didn't want it to devolve when they were this close to something. Hamilton didn't know what that something was, but her gut wrenched each time Solei opened her mouth. They were about to get a piece of evidence only Solei could give them, and that alone made it valuable. But first, the young woman had to say it out loud.

"My mother was with my father the day he died. Not at home, either. That morning, they argued about him going to see Marigold, but he left to meet her anyway. And… my mom… she followed him. She followed him to wherever he was meeting Marigold. She said the last time she saw my father alive was when they argued at the house, but she lied." Solei vomited her words, looking spent—anxious and mascara-streaked.

Hamilton's eyes grew wide. She stared in disbelief, trying to untangle her own thoughts. She glanced at her partner, who had finally stopped tapping his pencil and began chewing on the eraser end. She held his gaze, trying to signal him to ask the questions she couldn't. They both looked at Solei, who was weeping and wringing her hands under the table.

Rose finally asked, "Solei. What kind of car does your mother drive?"

Chapter 34

Hamilton

To his partner's annoyance, Rose grabbed the evidence bag with a little too much umph and left the room. Solei jumped at the abrupt departure, looking from Hamilton to the door. She could tell her partner's actions may have broken down the small bit of rapport they had built so far. Hamilton tried to recover by placing her hand on Solei's. She gave her a comforting look and said, "He can be a bit… rambunctious. We can verify that your mom followed your dad that day, but what makes you believe she did it? Did you see her there?"

"What? No. A friend of mine was driving by, and said they saw her. They only noticed because they saw my dad in his car, and my mother in hers across the street. They thought it was odd." Solei admitted. She began to sniffle and put her head down on the table.

"Alright Solei. Let's call it a day for now. I know this must be both physically and emotionally draining. Is there anything else you would like to share with us?" Hamilton asked gently. She waited intently for Solei to continue or ask to leave. Hamilton wanted to ask if they could take her fingerprints, but it might be counterintuitive. She had supplied evidence, more than once now, of her own volition. She didn't want to alienate Solei now, just in case there was more she could share. A few seconds passed, then Solei lifted her head and wiped tears from her cheeks.

"I need to know if it's true… if my mother followed him there. My friend has no reason to lie, but I guess I'm kind of hoping they were mistaken." Solei said.

"It will take us some time to look into it," Hamilton said, pausing, weighing the pros and cons once more about asking for fingerprints. "Solei, you've been a great help with this case. It's very important to us that we have the right person. There can't be any reasonable doubt about Marigold or anyone else's guilt. So, I need to ask for one more thing."

"Okay," Solei said, nervously.

"We found DNA and fingerprints… in an incriminating place. I want to be clear—I don't think you did this, so we need to rule you out. That would go a long way. It would be… very helpful. Would you consent to that?" Hamilton held her breath, trying to keep her face as measured as possible. What she didn't say was that, as the daughter of Luz, there would be some markers in Solei's DNA that could tie Luz to the letter.

"Yeah, whatever it takes," Solei responded, all hesitation absent from her voice.

As Hamilton grabbed kits for fingerprinting and DNA collection, she stopped to check with her partner.

Rose cradled a phone between his shoulder and ear, scribbling something down on a notepad. He held up the notepad just as the person on the line must have picked up, almost dropping the phone. "Yes, thank you, your honor." Then, slamming down the receiver, Rose hissed, "Yes! Got the greenlight on a warrant to get GPS records for Mrs. Quispe's car. Just for that day, but that's enough. Gonna get that ready, then head to IT. What are you up to?"

"Solei consented to fingerprints and DNA check," Hamilton replied, raising her eyebrows. They were finally making real strides in this cesspool of a case, and their anticipation was ratcheting upward. The two gave each other a non-verbal attaboy. She knew that adding another extremely viable suspect could present as problematic, but despite the body being in Hunter's car, her alibis were holding up. Luz on the other hand, didn't have an alibi they could speak of. The GPS could be enough for warrants to get anything else they needed. Those pieces of evidence were irrefutable, especially with the growing apparency of her motives. Hamilton felt for Solei. *It must be difficult to bring in evidence against your own mother.*

Marigold

Marigold jumped at the sound of a knock at her hospital room door. She assumed it was one of the nurses as she had asked her father not to visit her in the hospital… and the police never knocked.

"Come in," she said, annoyed at the pretense. To her surprise, a tall, lanky man with plastic hipster glasses peeked in. She couldn't help but notice his chiseled chin and angular cheeks, and the slim cut of his suit that made him look expensive all over. He had a 1950s side-parted haircut in his mahogany tresses, and eyes so blue they were almost clear. All at once, she felt self-conscious, smoothing her hair, and looking at him bewildered and intrigued. "Who are you?" she asked, noticing the police did not accompany him into the room as they did her other guests.

"Hi, Ms. Hunter. I'm Rudolpho Gutierrez. If you'll allow it, I've been hired to represent you. Specifically, your father hired me. You are also entitled to a public defender at no cost to you or your family. Do you understand? How would you like to proceed?" he asked with a deep, Spanish accent.

"Can we afford you?" she asked, both puzzled and a bit irritated with his unemotional introduction.

"Desmond said he has it handled. He and my father are old friends. I'm not doing it for free, but I am giving your family a great deal," he said.

Marigold didn't appreciate his candor but thought it may help her to have a shark in the courtroom. Despite her alibi, the reality was damning—the body was in her house, and she had put him in her trunk. There was no turning back now. She decided it was in her best interest to keep those two facts to herself—from the police and this new lawyer. Someone had already worked so hard to make her look guilty, she wasn't giving them or anyone else more ammunition.

Though Marigold questioned herself, she had an idea of what she was capable of, and decided murder wasn't one of those things. Something else dawned on her—she had loved Alberto; she could never kill him in cold blood. And now, everything was messed up.

The lawyer cleared his throat and Marigold was jostled out of her rabbit hole. "Sorry, yes, that's fine. Represent me," she replied, defeated. "So where do we go from here?" Marigold asked, looking him directly in the eyes though he towered over her sitting, wilted frame.

"May I," he asked, gesturing to a nearby chair. When Marigold nodded, he pulled the chair closer to her bed. "Next, we'll ask the judge to release you on your own recognizance. That is going to be very tough since the body was in your trunk, but—and this is not a question—you're simply being framed.

"From what my investigator has gathered so far, the body is the primary evidence the police have against you. Everything is circumstantial though motive is arguably there. We'll come back to that… and your relationship with Mr. Quispe. First, I've been able to schedule you a hearing for tomorrow. We'll have your father bring you some clothing—something neutral, sympathetic—and I will speak to the judge about releasing you to your father's care with outpatient psychological services."

Marigold wanted to be offended, to be outraged by his insinuation, but she did not trust herself either. She felt as if the last few months had been a delusion. How could she possibly have mistaken Alberto's affections for romantic when the man had thought she was his daughter all along? What did that say about the validity, the rationality of her thought process, her frame of reality? She'd spent every waking moment in this hospital replaying their encounters over and over, trying to discern a clue of some kind… trying to figure out when and how her mind twisted and perverted their friendship. Marigold looked down at her upturned palms, afraid to meet her lawyer's eyes.

After a beat, the lawyer continued. "Once you're out, you continue your counseling, and my team goes through whatever evidence the prosecutor may have. You are to have no contact with any of the Quispes. You are not to leave the state. You should also refrain from speaking with anyone about the case, including the police, unless I am present. We are the only two that will confer on your case. We're treading a fine line here and everything you say will be used against you. Can you agree to these terms? I'll preface by saying that if you cannot, I cannot work with you. I am not in the habit of sending my clients to prison," Gutierrez warned.

Their eyes met, and for one second, his blue eyes softened.

Marigold simply nodded.

Chapter 35

Hamilton

Hamilton walked Solei through fingerprinting and the swab for DNA, then hurriedly escorted her out of the station. She wanted to clear Solei. The young woman had lost her father, thought she had gained a sister, and now was under the impression her mother was a killer. To say she was dealt the rawest of hands didn't begin to cover it. Hamilton took a deep breath, then pushed into Gilbert's lab.

"Gilbert, can you compare these fingerprints to those on the envelope?" Hamilton requested. "Also, this lab test takes priority. Check it against the envelope as well, please. How long for the results?"

"If you want to hang for a minute, the fingerprints are pretty snappy. The DNA can take up to an hour, though," he said. His eyes darted over her and back to his screen.

She pulled up a wooden stool, eager to see the results. "I'm not sure the fingerprints will help as much, at least not with the envelope."

"Yeah, I know, but it's something. And they're good to have on hand to check against any other evidence we may find," Hamilton said, this time observing her colleague closely. She watched as he worked methodically even while carrying on a conversation. His work ethic was the one thing she liked about Gilbert. He got results; she couldn't deny that. Hamilton wondered how much she should share with him about her reservations—what her gut was yelling. She had her partner, but Monroe had a different knowledge base.

"Alright, so the fingerprints are on the envelope, but based on the pattern I feel I can safely say she didn't handle the envelope much. The DNA still has to work its magic, but again, it could take a while," he said.

Hamilton waited, sensing he wanted her to hang around. "Can I ask you a question? I'm thinking this DNA will not be a match, but… it could be close enough," Hamilton admitted.

Gilbert raised an eyebrow. "Elaborate?"

"Some evidence has come up that could suggest the wife is the killer. If that's true, then would there be enough similarities in the daughter's DNA—to say—make a judge more amenable to a warrant?" Hamilton asked.

"If the DNA from the envelope belongs to the mother, there will most definitely be enough markers to suggest a parental tie. Since we know Alberto didn't kill himself, it stands to reason that the DNA would belong to the other parent. Too bad Marigold is not his daughter. If she were, we could use Solei's DNA to confirm or rule her out," Gilbert suggested.

"True. That being said, if the wife has a lawyer with half a brain, this could keep us from getting that warrant," Hamilton replied.

She had an idea of what to do but couldn't show her hand quite yet. Hamilton smiled warmly at Gilbert, tapped his shoulder, and got up to leave the room. "Thanks. Do give me a call on my cell when the results are in."

As Hamilton made her way up to the office, she felt like they were on the right track. She rehashed all of the evidence, possible motives, and the circumstances of the car accident. Two things kept dinging in her mind. Why would a person cause an accident, knowing there was a body in their trunk? And who the hell sent the letter? There was the obvious reason that they knew the cause of death: hit and run. *Hmm, that's one way to hide evidence of such a case, but why not cause an accident after dumping the body—hide the evidence all around?*

Then something occurred to Hamilton. None of the witnesses mentioned anything about the condition of Hunter's car before the accident. They had nothing thus far to suggest that her car had sustained any previous damage. Forensics didn't find blood or hair in the front bumper. How could you have hit him hard enough to kill him? *We have the timeline: it's pretty tight to throw in a car detail.* "She's being framed," Hamilton muttered aloud as she pushed into the office department.

"Glad you're here," Rose greeted. "Grab some food?"

The two detectives made their way to the food trucks up the road. Hamilton peeked at her partner repeatedly, daring him to begin. Finally, Hamilton said, "Hunter is being framed," then paused to take in her partner's reaction. He simply smiled and nodded. Hamilton gave him the rundown about the lacking evidence. Rose nodded the entire time, adding in whistles and thigh slaps for effect.

"And Solei's DNA? What do we need that for?" he asked.

"Well, if the DNA has at least 50% matching markers, or whatever they're called, then we know the person that licked the envelope was Mrs. Quispe. And at this point, I don't even think there's a sibling. As Monroe said, 'we know it's not Alberto's.' I mean, I can't figure out why Luz would send such a letter, but she did lie about having it altogether," Hamilton said. "Then, there's GPS. I just know we're going to see that she followed her husband to that alley."

"Well, maybe the point of that letter was to embarrass Alberto," Rose suggested. "To get even. There's probably a love child out there somewhere, even if Hunter isn't it. I say, she sent that letter to get even with her husband, but it backfired. Once she realized, it was too late. She couldn't tell him it was all a trick—not if she wanted to keep him. Then… maybe… he found out and it all went to hell from there. Why Hunter… I don't know—"

The two found a table that was out of earshot of the other diners and ate in silence, devouring their wraps as they waited anxiously to hear about the lab results.

They needed all the evidence they could get. Hamilton cared most about exonerating an innocent young woman, while she was certain that Rose was focused on getting the killer.

Just as Hamilton was about to speak, the table buzzed, making them both jump. The partners looked at each other, reaching for their phones before they saw that it was Hamilton's call to answer.

"Hamilton here," she greeted, waiting for the voice on the other line.

"The DNA on the envelope is not Solei's—but based on the markers, it has to be her parent. What do you need me to do?" Gilbert asked.

"Make sure the case number is attached and send me a secure email with the results. We're getting another warrant," Hamilton replied, then ended the call. She looked up at Rose. "The DNA has to belong to the wife." Hamilton stood up to leave, nodding at her partner.

As they walked back to the station, she sighed. "Why did that feel so damn anticlimactic?"

"I'm sorry, but hey—it's something," Rose said. "That DNA connects Mrs. Quispe with Hunter, plus motive, the deceased Quispe's agenda, and hopefully, the GPS results. With the body being found in Hunter's trunk, we need all the evidence we can get to charge someone else," Rose said.

"And at the very least—keep Hunter out of prison for a crime she didn't commit," Hamilton said, relieved. Her partner wasn't the type to assuage anyone's feelings—especially those he cared about. So, his reassurance held more weight. Hamilton smiled at Rose. "Let's go pay IT a visit."

***

As the detectives stood over the IT crime technician, they whispered to each other. The technician periodically peeked over his shoulder, giving the two a dirty look, but they ignored him.

Hunter had a hearing the next day, and they wanted to have someone else to take into custody before she was released.

"Okay. We got it. It looks like this vehicle followed our victim to the café, they stopped, then followed the victim to the scene of the crime," he said.

"And? Can you see how long she was there… or rather, did she stop or keep going? I mean can you see that?" Rose asked.

"We can't see the finer details, but it looks like her car was stopped there… hold on. Yes, it stopped there shortly after his did, and she didn't move again until… ten minutes later—"

Hamilton cut him off. "That's enough time to hit him, drag him into the trunk, and drive off," Hamilton said, clicking her tongue.

"Hot damn!" Rose blurted.

"Wait. Where did she go after?" Hamilton asked.

"Ah, Hamilton, you had to ruin the moment," Rose said.

"She went to… 566 Chase Road," the tech replied, looking at them inquisitively.

"Pretty sure that's their house. Did she go anywhere else?" Hamilton asked, opening her notebook. She slipped through a few pages and pointed. "Specifically, to this address."

The tech clicked away. "Sorry, not in this window of time," he said, disappointed.

"That's okay, that's okay. We still have her following the husband, stopping there at the scene of the crime, then driving off minutes later," Rose said, triumphantly, "The only warrant we need now is for an arrest."

Chapter 36

The Next Day

Marigold

Marigold stood beside her lawyer in a tan, high-neck dress. She stared blankly at the judge, unable to absorb his words. He said something that amused her lawyer, but her mind spiraled in panic. If things didn't work the way the lawyer projected, she'd be carted off to jail.

The memory of Alberto's dead body kept resurfacing. Every time she closed her eyes, she saw him and the deep, wide gash on his head.

The sound of someone clearing their throat, followed by a loud thump, brought her back. Marigold looked up at the judge, who was leaning forward and staring at her oddly.

"Good day, Ms. Hunter. I trust your lawyer can help you find your way out," the judge said before he left the courtroom.

"What? What's happened?" Marigold asked, bewildered.

"It would behoove you to pay attention when in court. You were only suspected of murder, Ms. Hunter," Rudolpho said, shaking his head. "What's happened is the charges have been dropped. It would seem they've caught the right person."

Marigold's eyes filled with tears; it felt unreal. She whipped around to look for confirmation from her father. He stood there on the pew behind hers, smiling, arms stretched out to gather her up. Tentatively, she stepped toward him, then collapsed into his arms.

Solei

Solei and Camila watched as Luz rummaged through Alberto's desk in a rage. "*Pinche pendeja* isn't getting our family's money," Luz muttered.

As Luz tore through each drawer, she didn't bother closing them. Papers and folders fluttered to the floor as she desperately emptied drawer after drawer for paperwork—proof of paternity, any sign of a previous will. The crisp lines of her pressed suit stood in stark contrast to her flushed face and blood-red palms. Her hair was swooped neatly into a side pony with a long braid falling down her left side, but her face was streaked with tears and mascara.

She spun around again and again. As Luz turned for the third time, she caught a glimpse of herself in an art déco mirror on the far wall. Her reflection made her jump. She rushed to the bathroom, glanced at her watch, allowed herself exactly two minutes to cry, then scrubbed furiously at her face with a wet napkin.

Three cars pulled into the small parking lot of the Quispes' flagship perfume shop, *Bajo Del Sol*. Solei flinched at the sight of the uniformed cop and the detectives emerging. It was all happening too quickly, and she didn't know what to do. She caught Hamilton's eyes and grabbed Camila's arm as if to brace herself.

"Just wait," she said, her voice barely above a whisper.

Camila looked at her, the corners of her lips twitching. Her expression gave Solei pause, but her attention snapped back as Luz was escorted out of the shop in handcuffs. Their clerk trailed behind, crying dramatically.

Solei froze. That should have been her crying behind her mother, but all she felt was confusion. Though she had brought the police information, a big part of her didn't want it to be true.

"I just… I can't believe it. This can't be happening," Solei whispered, not daring to look over at her best friend. *Do I call her a lawyer? Do I follow the police?* Her thoughts were a mixture of empathy, disgust, and bewilderment.

She glanced at Camila, hoping her best friend would tell her what to do next, but Camila's gaze was fixed on Luz.

In the second before she got into her vehicle, Hamilton looked over at Solei; their eyes met for several long seconds.

Solei watched as the two cars pulled away with her mother in custody, then stepped out without saying a word. She put her arms around the weeping clerk and ushered her back inside to help close the shop. Camila was immobile, standing in the doorway, watching, hands pressed into fists.

Chapter 37

Luz

This is just offensive. Luz took in the large slabs of gray concrete in the tight, musty room. The cold stung her bare body as the hands of the stranger in a prison guard uniform invaded her space. Her wrists chafed and burned. She fought not to squirm against the calluses of her invader's skin. The whimper at the tip of her tongue threatened to escape, but she refused. *I'm not a barbarian,* she thought, silently protesting the animal indignity of the experience.

This was the exact life she had avoided, and yet it paralleled the one she had endured until now—the one she had feigned to enjoy. A life of being summoned at others' pleasures, of presenting herself on demand, of putting on dignity no matter the situation.

And who was summoning her now? Alberto was gone; he no longer demanded her time, her perfection, the decorum he grew to resent. And what was her beloved Solei thinking, feeling? As her clothes were pulled back to cover her shamed, naked frame, Luz hoped for her daughter. But with every step on the long guilt-ridden walk toward her summoner, she knew, deep down, it wouldn't be Solei.

Once in the dismal visiting room, a melding of concrete and metal, Luz sat with her back straight, chin up, burning and thrashing inside. When she thought her façade would collapse into her real self, the doors slid open with a clank, and a vision appeared. For a second, she thought it was *Solei*—maybe the result of her longing.

"God doesn't like ugly, Mrs. Ramirez-Quispe," Camila said, entering the visiting room, her eyes wide and menacing.

Luz stared at her, puzzled. Camila smiled, bearing perfect teeth.

"Five years of dealing with your daughter's emotional instability—and suffering your dictatorship. Ugh!" Camila glowered at Luz. "Still don't know who I am? No… you don't recognize *her* face in mine. Your husband didn't either. It doesn't matter—my mother is dead and so is your husband. Do you know how hard it is to move a body?" Camila burst into a full, hearty laugh and leaned close until her face nearly touched Luz's.

"All you had to do was share your family… and all I had to do was write a letter on behalf of my dearly departed mother, River. Now if you don't mind, I have a psychiatric file to return."

Luz's heart raced and sweat beaded at the base of her neck. She tried to speak, but she choked on her words. Memories clicked in freeze-frame motion as her eyes darted around the space. *Camila!* Luz stumbled backward, her head on a swivel, but there was nowhere to hide. When her back hit the concrete wall, the cold crawled over her skin. Luz shrank down to the floor. She scraped the nails of her left hand into her right, longing for the heat of shame to replace the cold fear of the truth. Yet the revelation of her visitor's true identity swelled, until finally, several drops of blood burst through her wounded palm.

The End

ABOUT THE AUTHOR

Nicole Negrón is a novelist, teaching artist, and museum educator from Jersey City, New Jersey. Her published works include "A Dream," "Faith and Dandelion Seeds," "Evermore," "Tether," "Unrequited," and many more. Nicole writes mysteries, domestic drama, and speculative fiction centered on family, women, and BIPOC communities. She is passionate about writing, reading, and providing accessible, educational enrichment experiences for the community. Nicole earned a Bachelor of Arts in English and History from Misericordia University, along with master's degrees in Museum Studies from Johns Hopkins University and Fiction Writing from Wilkes University. When she isn't writing or reading, she's spending time with her family or enjoying all things stationery.